CHA

The low autumn sun dazzled the calm sea into a sheet of brilliance. Jinny Manders, balancing easily on the back of her rearing Arab mare, was silhouetted against its light.

'Easy Shantih,' Jinny whispered, feeling her horse plunging and dancing, desperate to gallop on over the stretching sands. 'Steady now.'

Jinny held Shantih with the lightest touch on her bit, controlling her between hands and seat. Jinny's fingers felt the reins as if they were living strands that brought all the energy of the chestnut mare under her command.

'Steady,' she whispered again and then, relaxing her hold, she released Shantih.

For a split second Jinny felt the power of her horse massed beneath her; felt Shantih held, both arrow and bow, by her own tension and then she was away. Neck stretched out; mane and tail bannered by her speed, the piston beat of Shantih's hooves thudded into the shimmering sands. The great muscles of Shantih's shoulders and quarters strained beneath the red-gold sheen of her satin skin. Her head with its dished muzzle, flaunting nostrils and dark-silver eyes dared into space in an ecstasy of galloping. Jinny crouched low over Shantih's withers, her hands on either side of Shantih's neck. Her own red-gold hair streamed out from beneath her hard hat and her tight, bony knees were welded against the saddle.

'Faster,' she shouted. 'On you go, on you go.'

As the wind of their speed ripped the sound from

Jinny's lips she felt her horse surge forward. She rode now in a blur of speed. Sea, sand and sky were one. Only the gulls' fishwife screaming was separate; clear beyond their flight.

But it wasn't enough. Not enough to blot out the black mood that crouched on Jinny's shoulders, holding on with knotted, monkey fingers as it whispered into her mind, 'School tomorrow, school tomorrow, school tomorrow.'

Reaching the far side of the bay, Jinny brought Shantih to a spring-hoofed trot.

'Where now?' Shantih demanded with tossing head, clinking bit and prancing forefeet.

Without hesitation Jinny turned her at the sheep track that angled upward to the fields beyond Mr MacKenzie's farm. Normally when Jinny took this track she rode cautiously, giving Shantih her head so that she could pick her own way up the almost vertical ladder of crumbling, sandy soil and boulders. But today she urged Shantih on, delighting in the strength of her horse; in seeing Shantih dig her toes into the soft earth and fight her way upwards.

Even when Shantih missed her footing and for a moment Jinny felt the clutch of gravity that could pluck them from the track and send them hurtling down to the sands below, she didn't care. It was what she wanted. She wanted danger and excitement; wanted to fill the afternoon with action to stop herself thinking of going back to school tomorrow; of the weeks and weeks of boredom that lay ahead. The Christmas holidays were so far away they couldn't even be imagined.

'Fit horse,' praised Jinny as Shantih burst from the confines of the track on to the open moorland. 'I could ride you in a steeplechase and you wouldn't even notice. You could jump the moon and the stars and the wall in the

Puissance at The Horse of The Year show. That would be something worth doing. Not boring old school. Boring, boring school. How I hate it.'

Beneath Jinny, Finmory Bay had dwindled into a toy bay with its neat loop of water and arc of sand, held in the black jaws of rock. Across the fields was Mr MacKenzie's farm, and beyond the farm, closer to the bay, was Finmory House where Jinny lived. It was a grey stone house, standing four-square and rooted. Its front windows looked out over garden grounds, past the field where Jinny kept Shantih and on to the bay. Behind the house a wilderness of moorland stretched to mountains bulked black against the sky. And that was all. Mountains, moor and sea. Jinny loved it with all her being. Asked only to be allowed to go on living there forever, free to gallop Shantih, to paint and draw, knowing that Finmory House and her family were always there.

Two years ago the Manders family – Mr and Mrs Manders; Petra, Jinny's elder sister who was sixteen, and Mike, Jinny's younger brother who was eleven – had all lived in Stopton, a city of endless traffic and vibrating noise. Mr Manders had been a probation officer until he became so disillusioned that he had decided to become a potter, had bought Finmory House and brought them all to live in the north-west of Scotland.

Petra was a weekly boarder at Duninver High School. Jinny went to Inverburgh Comprehensive, riding Shantih into Glenbost, the nearest village, and leaving her there during the day while she caught the school bus into Inverburgh. Until now Mike had ridden Bramble, a black Highland pony borrowed from Miss Tuke's trekking centre, into Glenbost, leaving him in the field with Shantih, while he attended the village school. Now he was starting at

Inverburgh Comprehensive and would be setting off every morning with Jinny.

'Boring, boring, boring school,' Jinny repeated aloud.

At the back of her mind there was something that made it more than boring. Something that had happened at the end of last term. It hadn't mattered then because the summer holidays were starting, her return to school in September had been a lifetime away and Jinny hadn't cared. Now she couldn't remember what it was; only knew there was something waiting for her.

'Better take a look at your term-time field,' she said to Shantih and, closing her legs against Shantih's sides, she trotted off in the direction of Glenbost. The village consisted of Mrs Simpson's shop, two churches, a garage and a primary school, all surrounded by a cluster of crofts.

As she trotted along, Jinny's black mood settled in on her. It was like a cold, wet cloak that wrapped itself round her, blinkering out the bright day.

'Not as bad as Stopton,' Jinny said, struggling to free herself from its grip. 'And I'd have been going back to school there too.'

Suddenly Shantih snorted, shied violently as a hoodie crow erupted from the heather and was cantering down the road before Jinny had recovered her seat.

'Fine day,' called Mrs Simpson from her shop doorway.

'School tomorrow,' answered Jinny in a voice of doom.

'Now do not be grumbling at that. When I was your age and younger, I was down on my knees all day scrubbing the floors for the gentry.'

'Wouldn't have liked that either,' agreed Jinny.

'Indeed and you would not.'

'But it doesn't make school any better.'

'It is grateful you should be for the chance to be at the

education. All those books and not a penny to be paid for them. Wasted you are with so much handed to you on plates.'

At the mention of school books the monkey voice chattered more clearly in Jinny's head but still she couldn't remember, couldn't quite hear what it was saying.

'And it is your brother will be for Inverburgh school this term?'

'He's looking forward to it. Doesn't know what's waiting for him.'

'Och, he's got more sense to him than you'll ever have and that is a sure thing.'

'You could be right there,' agreed Jinny, thinking how Mike had spent his summer helping Mr MacKenzie on the farm, learning to drive the tractor, to milk the cows and to work Betsy, Mr MacKenzie's sheepdog. 'He wants to be a farmer.'

'There's the sensible thing now. Could you not settle yourself to something the same? You're too old to be carrying on with your nonsenses.'

'Thirteen,' said Jinny. 'Old age pension, here I come. Actually I'm thinking of being a village shopkeeper. Seems like a nice hobby.'

'Get away with you,' said Mrs Simpson, not amused.

'Have to check the horses' field,' said Jinny, riding on.

'It will be pleasant having their company again. Many's the wee word I have with them through the day. And it is the more civil tongue the poor dumb beasts have in their heads than those who own them,' called Mrs Simpson, getting the last word.

'Be nice for you not having to wait on your own for me to come home,' Jinny said as she led Shantih round the field, checking the hedges in case they should have developed any horse-sized gaps, and searching the grass for any glass or wire. 'Now Mike is coming to Inverburgh we'll all be able to ride home together. That is when I'm not in detention. The few little wee times when I am not in detention.' Again Jinny almost remembered what it was that had happened at the end of last term. Almost but not quite.

Jinny found two lemonade bottles which made her search worthwhile, but no holes in the hedge. The open shed that sheltered both horses and tack was still sound and rainproof.

Shutting the field gate behind herself, Jinny was about to mount Shantih when Mr Simpson appeared round the corner of the hedge. Shantih sprang away in mock terror, eyes goggling, tail high.

'Och, it is not one bit better she is,' declared Mr Simpson, putting down the box he was carrying and stopping to watch Jinny struggling to calm Shantih down. 'Wild as the heather that one.'

'She is not!' exclaimed Jinny. 'It was you creeping up on us like that. Shantih's a million times better than when I got her at first.'

'Well, maybe the fraction improved from when she was running wild on the moors after Jock MacKenzie had bought her from the circus.'

'You could be right there,' said Jinny.

'Now I knew there was something I had to tell you – a wee thing my brother was after telling me. It's over on the east coast he lives, and a few weeks ago there was a nasty accident at his very door. A circus van crashing into his wall and the driver taken off to the hospital.'

At the mention of a circus a shiver had run through Jinny. When they had first come to Finmory the Manders had spent their first night in an Inverburgh hotel and Mr Manders had taken Mike and Jinny to a travelling circus. It had been a third rate circus but the last act had been Shantih, billed then as Yasmin the Killer Horse. She had been trained to rear up and lash out with her forefeet when the ringmaster whipped her. Jinny had watched with utter horror and then dashed from her seat and flung herself at the ringmaster, screaming at him to stop.

Driving back to the hotel that night had been one of the blackest depths in Jinny's life. She loved the chestnut Arab, totally and forever, but there had seemed nothing she could do to save her from the circus.

'Now it was after the accident,' continued Mr Simpson, 'My brother was hearing the interview on the radio with the ringmaster. And I'm thinking it must have been the very same circus as the one her ladyship came from, for was he not telling the interviewer how one of his vans had been in a crash before and how his valuable Arab horse had escaped on to the moors and him not able to catch her.'

In an instant Jinny relived the day – three days after they had visited the circus, – when the circus van loaded with Shantih and two other horses had crashed with a lorry on the Inverburgh road, Jinny and Mr MacKenzie had been watching from the hillside. They had raced down to the accident in time to see Shantih break out from the wreckage and gallop to freedom over the moors.

'And here's the strange thing,' continued Mr Simpson. 'The ringmaster seemed to think that when he was back in this district he would be reclaiming his horse. And us all believing Jock MacKenzie had bought her from the circus and it was yourself had bought her from Jock.'

Jinny stared in horror at Mr Simpson. She burst out, 'Of

course Mr MacKenzie bought Shantih from the circus and I bought her from him. Of course she belongs to me!'

Mr Simpson pondered Jinny's indignation. 'Then maybe my brother was not listening too carefully,' he said. 'Maybe the ringmaster was saying he would be buying her back.'

'As if I would ever sell Shantih!' exclaimed Jinny scornfully.

Turning away from Mr Simpson Jinny swung herself into the saddle. She wished she had never met Mr Simpson. It was all the day had needed – the thought of the ringmaster coming to Finmory and trying to buy Shantih back.

After Shantih had escaped from the circus van she had roamed the moors for months, refusing to let anyone near her. Only when Jinny had found her, close to death, in a snow blizzard, had she been able to bring her back to Finmory.

'I would NEVER sell Shantih!'

'Maybe not,' said Mr Simpson. 'But if there's money in it for himself I'm thinking Jock MacKenzie could fix anything.'

'It has nothing to do with him. I bought Shantih from him. She's mine.'

It was true Jinny had bought Shantih, but she had only paid sixty pounds for her and given Mr KacKenzie two of her paintings. When Jinny thought about it, it did not seem anything like enough for an Arab mare. So little, in fact, that Mr MacKenzie might feel that he still had a claim on Shantih.

Jinny rode towards Finmory and then checked herself. To ride straight home meant she was back at school. Nothing more would happen between now and being at school. Jinny didn't want that. She wanted excitement and danger; things to make her feel alive; happenings that would make tomorrow seem centuries away. Riding home wouldn't make anything happen. She had to think of something dangerous to do; force herself to do something of which she was afraid.

Jinny thought of Miss Tuke's cross country course but there was not even time to dream of hacking to Miss Tuke's. There was a dreaded drop jump on the moors. Jinny had jumped it twice. You rode down a steep slope, jumped the three foot wall, then dropped through space, down and down a lift shaft of nothing until you reached the ground, still sloping away on the landing.

'That would do,' decided Jinny, feeling her stomach clench at the thought. Then she remembered that Mr MacKenzie and two of his sons were on the hill with the sheep. 'Don't want them watching me. Bound to come off if they're about.'

Shantih bounded impatiently, stretched her neck for grass, then took instant advantage of the length of rein to swing round and trot for home.

'Got it,' cried Jinny, gathering up her reins and turning Shantih in the opposite direction. 'I'll ride along the Inverburgh road as far as the track over the moor that brings us back to Glenbost. That will waken us up. Shan't have time to think about bloomin' school when I'm dodging the lorries.'

Jinny trotted Shantih briskly along the empty road from Glenbost towards the Inverburgh road. It wound through waves of gilded bracken and glowing outbursts of purple heather. Tattered sheep were mounded in the shelter of vast boulders of grey rock, and on top of the boulders crows stretched feathered necks to watch them pass.

Turning out on to the Inverburgh road Shantih fretted and baulked. She wanted to go home, not to be ridden on towards Inverburgh when the late afternoon shadows were stretching down from the mountains and the air losing its brightness. She pirouetted on the road, fighting Jinny, her hooves scoring the tarmacadam.

The road to Inverburgh was always busy. One side of it was fenced, the other side a mass of boulders, so that once Jinny was riding along it, she had to go on until she reached the track that led back over the hills to Glenbost.

A car skidded to a halt behind them as an articulated lorry thundered past on the other side of the road.

Jinny sat close and tight, urging Shantih on with her seat and legs, remembering not to use her heels, as she felt Shantih drop behind her bit and threaten to rear.

'Get on with you,' Jinny muttered between clenched teeth. 'Idiot. Break your knees if you come down on this.'

Shantih's front feet lifted in a half rear, the driver of the car stuck behind them sounded his horn and Shantih shot forward. The car roared past them and was out of sight before Jinny managed to control Shantih's gallop into a raking, unbalanced trot. But Jinny was not thinking about school. The thought of tomorrow had vanished from her mind.

The track back to Glenbost had just come into sight when a long distance coach drew out to pass Shantih. The passengers looked out curiously. Jinny, used to people in cars and buses staring at her when she was riding hardly noticed them until she saw a young man jump up from his seat and begin to wave to her. Concentrating on controlling Shantih, Jinny grinned at him, not daring to take her hand off the reins. The young man's waving became more frantic. He was struggling to open the top section of the window, his face close to the glass, his lips mouthing words that Jinny couldn't possibly hear.

Two cars came speeding towards the coach, forcing it to draw back behind Jinny again. Shantih laid her ears, switched her tail and lashed out with a peevish hind hoof. Jinny stared fixedly ahead dreading to hear the sound of tinkling glass as the coach's headlight smashed to the ground. But there was no sound. Shantih had missed it.

'Fool horse,' cursed Jinny nervously. 'Behave yourself.'

Seeing the road clear again, the coach roared forward. The young man had managed to open the window and with his face jammed in the narrow opening he was yelling at her.

'Where did you buy your horse?' he shouted at Jinny as the coach carried him past.

An electric shiver zigzagged down Jinny's spine. She could see clearly in her mind's eye the man's hard, pale blue eyes, sharp nose and pointed chin.

'Nothing to do with him,' she thought. 'Shantih's mine and that is all there is to it. MINE.'

The dread of Shantih ever being taken from her filled Jinny's mind as she urged Shantih across the road and along the uphill track that led back to Glenbost.

'Who was he?' Jinny thought, as she eased her hands on the reins and felt Shantih change from a trot to a gliding canter. 'Why should he want to know where I bought you? Sticking his stupid head out of the bus window like that,' and Jinny rode Shantih at the first of the dry stone walls that ribbed the moorland.

Jinny had whitewashed a course for herself so that she was able to ride on over the walls, knowing that if she kept to the whitewashed stones there was a clear landing on the other side of the wall. In actual fact, sheep scrabbling over the walls often knocked down stones and usually Jinny checked, but today she cantered on, following the bright blobs of whitewash, jumping each wall as she came to it. Shantih, with Finmory ahead of her, sailed over the walls in fluid arcs, ears pricked, hooves tucked close to her body as she cleared the low walls with feet to spare.

By the time the young man had managed to persuade the coach driver to stop and let him off, and had raced back to where he had seen the girl and the chestnut Arab ride on to the moor, Jinny and Shantih were tiny toy figures, almost invisible against the camouflage of autumn russets and gold.

The young man cupped his hands to his mouth and roared at the pitch of his lungs.

'Come back! Come back! I want to speak to you. You on the Arab, come back! Tell me where you found her.'

But not the least whisper of his urgent demand reached Jinny as she galloped on.

Shrugging his shoulders hopelessly, the young man stood watching until both horse and rider had disappeared from sight. There was nothing more he could do. He couldn't start to track the horse over the moors for soon it would be too dark to see.

'I'm sure it's her,' he muttered to himself as he walked back to the road. 'Bloomin' certain. I'd know that mare anywhere, even after all this time.'

CHAPTER TWO

'Dougal won't wait,' snapped Jinny.

Irritated almost beyond endurance by Mike's enthusiasm for starting a new school Jinny had gorged down her porridge, toast and coffee, and was now waiting impatiently for Mike to finish his breakfast.

'Dougal's not the sort of driver to keep the school bus waiting for us if we're not on time. So get a move on.'

'Oh, Jinny, calm yourself,' said her mother, thinking that much as she loved Jinny she would be more than delighted to see her safely on her way to school. Jinny had spent the evening before moaning and procrastinating, and when Mrs Manders had been on the point of losing her temper with her, had insisted that she had to go out and check up on Shantih. 'You've half an hour before you need to be away. Plenty of time. You're not usually so worried about missing the bus.'

'Dougal will go without us,' Jinny repeated, gripping the back of Mike's chair and rocking it backward and forward. 'And it won't be my fault.'

'Stop it! He won't go without *me*. So there.'

'He will. Go without anyone. Drive the bus empty to Inverburgh if we were all late.'

'Not *me*. He'll wait for me.'

'Won't.'

'Will.'

'Won't. Bloomin' well won't. And I should know. I've been trailing in and out for a whole year on that rattle-bone, tin can of a bus.'

'Danny starts at Inverburgh to-day. He's my friend and Dougal is his Uncle. So they won't go without me.' Mike stretched out a casual hand for another slice of toast.

Jinny glared at her brother. Despite herself she felt the corners of her mouth twitching into a smile.

'See,' said Mike. 'You'll be O.K. now you've got me.'

Had it been Petra – bossy, always right, perfect Petra – Jinny would have been furious. But Mike was different. Jinny couldn't stop herself grinning at him.

'Just for once, seeing it's your first day, I'll tack Bramble up for you,' she said.

'Right.'

Jinny gathered up her school bag, hard hat and plastic carrier bag containing her school skirt. She dragged on her riding mack, grabbed up her belongings and blitzed out into the steady drizzle.

Ken Dawson with his grey dog, Kelly, was waiting at the stable. Ken was nineteen. He was lean and bony, with fair hair growing to his shoulders. He lived with the Manders, helping Mr Manders in the pottery, making pots that were far better than Mr Manders' work, and growing fruit and vegetables for them all.

'"Shades of the prison house"?' Ken quoted.

'All right for you,' said Jinny, dumping her things down on the stable floor. 'You do nothing all day.'

'I know,' agreed Ken. 'They packed me off to prep school when I was seven, they were so desperate to get rid of me.'

When Ken had lived in Stopton he had been put on probation because he had been with other boys who had broken into a warehouse. At the end of his probation he had assured Mr Manders that he had had nothing to do with the break-in. 'I know,' Mr Manders had acknowledged.

But his parents had wanted nothing more to do with their son. They were well off but, except for sending him a monthly cheque, they had washed their hands of him.

When Ken had arrived at Finmory, all the family had welcomed his help, especially Jinny. Ken understood the way she felt. When she showed Ken her drawings he said the right things about them, not embarrassing praise or condescending amazement. When Jinny had been lost on the Finmory moors in a snow blizzard, it had been Ken who had found her and saved her life. Ken was the only person Jinny knew who really loved animals. He didn't use them or eat them or turn them into pampered pets. He shared his world with them as equals.

Ken leaned over the door of Shantih's loose box, watching Jinny grooming.

'Weeks and months of prison,' Jinny moaned.

'Stop it,' commanded Ken. 'Change the channel. You are about to go for a ride on your own Arab. What more could you possibly want?'

'To name but a few . . .' said Jinny.

Ken swung away. 'Be that way if you want,' he said.

'Do want,' said Jinny. 'You'd be like this if you had to go back to school. Don't kid yourself.'

But Ken had broken her blackness. Riding to Glenbost with Mike, she couldn't help knowing how good it was to be trotting Shantih through the awakening morning; couldn't help being aware of Bramble's bustling, bright-eyed presence as Mike urged him on to keep up with Shantih.

It wasn't until the school bus was rattling them into Inverburgh that Jinny sank back into her sullen rebellion. Beside her, Dolina, who was in her class at school, chatted on about Adrian her summer boyfriend and Jinny stared through the bus window. The early drizzle had changed into heavy rain. Hunchbacked under their umbrellas, Inverburgh workers thronged the pavements. The rain turned roads and pavements into gleaming whale-backs and cars glistened gaudily against the grey.

'Were you remembering the essay for history?' Dolina asked smugly. 'It's Adrian will be studying the history at the university next year, so I'm thinking I'll be getting twenty out of twenty for mine.'

'I've done it but I dare say I'll get minus twenty for it,' began Jinny but stopped suddenly.

Surrounded by posters advertising soap and cars and beer there was a poster covered with clowns, spangled ladies and prancing, plumed white horses. It was a poster advertising a circus.

'Let me out quick,' Jinny yelled, fighting her way past Dolina, racing up the bus to the door.

'If it is sick you are going to be,' said Dougal, 'be holding it in until we reach the school.'

The automatic doors of the bus had long since jammed open, so that Jinny was able to cling to the metal bar, leaning out as far as she was able, trying desperately to see the circus poster more clearly. It was certainly a poster advertising a circus but she couldn't make out the dates announcing when it was coming to Inverburgh; couldn't read the name of the circus.

'Get in with you,' shouted Dougal, 'and be seating yourself back down when I tell you.'

'I've got to get off,' Jinny shouted back, but the bus was going too fast, the traffic packed too closely around it for Jinny to have jumped off.

'Sit down!' roared Dougal and Jinny sank back into the nearest seat.

'Please take my bags,' Jinny pleaded with Dolina as they

stood inside the school gates. 'I must go and see that poster. Got to know if the circus is coming this week.'

And with a cold clutch of fear Jinny thought about the man who had been on the coach. Had he something to do with the circus? Had the ringmaster told him to be on the lookout for a chestnut Arab?

'Would you be listening to me,' said Dolina standing rooted, pale cod-eyes staring straight at Jinny from her full-moon face. 'I'm having no more of you this term. It's full of the rubbish you are and it is enough of it I have been having.'

Jinny dumped her bags at Dolina's feet.

'Well leave them there,' she said furiously, 'and you can draw your own maps this term.'

The sound of the bell electrified the crowds of children into action. Shouting, running, pushing, dawdling reluctantly they flowed into lines; only Jinny, head down, raced in the opposite direction. She had to find out when the circus was coming to Inverburgh; had to know.

Not pausing she charged through the school gates, straight into the substantial bulk of Miss Lorimer, her last year's Guidance mistress.

'Jinny Manders!' Miss Lorimer exclaimed, staggering under the force of Jinny's assault. 'Where do you think you're going?'

'I've got . . .'

'You've got to get into line.' With Miss Lorimer's heavy hand on her shoulder Jinny was steered back into school.

'Mr Kirby is your Register teacher this year, isn't he?'

Jinny, considering the consequences of wriggling her way to freedom had no idea who her new Register teacher would be.

'I've got to go and see a circus poster,' she muttered. 'They could be trying to take Shantih.'

If Miss Lorimer heard her she chose to ignore her.

'Tell him,' she said, 'that when he has finished with you I want to see you in my room as soon as possible. I looked for you at the end of last term but no one seemed to be able to tell me where you were.'

Miss Lorimer guided Jinny to the front of her line.

'Now, do you understand? I want to see you in my room whenever Mr Kirby has finished with you,' she said, accentuating her words with an ill-natured jerk at Jinny's coat.

'Child molester,' thought Jinny, as she dashed across the playground to where her bags lay abandoned.

'You were quick,' said Dolina when Jinny joined her in the line.

'You were rotten mean leaving all my stuff just lying there. Friend? Huh, some friend!'

'It is to learn you that you cannot go running off and expect me to be covering up for you.'

'Teach,' said Jinny. 'Teach, not learn.'

'What happened to you that you're back like the boomerang?'

'Bumped into the Lorry. Wants me in her room, sooner than now.'

'It's popular you are in this school,' said Dolina. 'And what would she be wanting you for?'

'How should I know?'

Even when she was standing outside Miss Lorimer's door, half an hour later, her hand raised to knock on the frosted glass, Jinny still had no idea what she could have done wrong.

'Come in,' called Miss Lorimer's voice as Jinny wondered if there might be time for her to sneak out through the gap in the school fencing and see the poster before the first lesson.

On Miss Lorimer's immaculate desk was a pile of textbooks. Jinny recognised them as the ones her class had used last year. Looking at them more closely she saw her name on a tattered, brown paper cover. They were her books, and instantly Jinny remembered what it was that had been nagging at the back of her mind; the thing that she hadn't done at the end of last term.

Without speaking, Miss Lorimer opened the books one by one. She laid them in front of Jinny and leafed through them. On page after page Shantih grazed and galloped. Her wide eyes gazed up at Jinny from flowing mane and forelock; details of hooves and hocks filled margins. Shantih cavorted around geometry diagrams and blank end papers were graced with her rearing beauty.

'Well?' said Miss Lorimer.

'I forgot my rubber,' said Jinny. 'I bought a new one, honestly I did. Then Mike borrowed it and when I got to school he hadn't put it back in my bag.'

'You bought a new rubber,' Miss Lorimer echoed scornfully. 'Is that all you have to say for yourself?'

'But I did! I meant to rub it all out.'

'The point is,' stated Miss Lorimer, 'you should not have been drawing on school textbooks in the first place. This is not the first time I have had to speak to you about scribbling on school books but this . . .! This is the most blatant disregard for school property . . .'

Jinny stopped listening. In her mind's eye the young man on the coach had tracked her down to Glenbost and had discovered Shantih, unguarded in her field. Jinny saw him hold out peppermints to Shantih, saw her horse stepping towards him, bending her head to take the sweets as the man dropped a halter rope over her neck.

If he was from the circus, Jinny was sure that he would

stop at nothing to get Shantih back. Perhaps he had already told the ringmaster, and Jinny saw Mr MacKenzie's eyes glistening with greed as he listened to the ringmaster's offer to buy Shantih back. She heard his voice smiling on the ringmaster.

'Now it was nothing but a wee agreement between the lassie and myself,' she heard him say. 'She gave me the wee touch money to be having the use of the horse until yourself was coming to buy her back. I'll be speaking to her this very evening.'

'I must find out if it is the same circus,' Jinny thought desperately.

'Are you listening to me?'

Jinny swam back to Miss Lorimer's room, to the spread of opened textbooks.

'Yes,' she lied. 'And I am sorry. I did mean to rub it all out. It was Mike's fault. I bought . . .'

'You mentioned it,' stated Miss Lorimer. 'Well if you've nothing else to say for yourself I want you here at lunchtime. "I must not deface school property" one hundred times. Bring your rubber tomorrow and clean up this mess.'

'I can't stay in at lunchtime,' began Jinny.

'Can and will,' said Miss Lorimer. 'I'm only giving you the chance to do your lines at lunchtime so that you don't have to stay in after school. I know you have a long way to travel.'

'I can't . . .'

'Now back to Mr Kirby. I'll check up with him that you have gone straight back,' Miss Lorimer added, as she looked at her watch.

Full of gobbled-down school dinner, Jinny sat at Miss Lorimer's desk. She wrote, "I must not deface school property," twenty three times, writing it in columns – twenty three "Is", twenty three "musts" – until she came to the end of the sentence.

Then she opened her last year's French book and looked at her drawings. One of Shantih with her ears back was exactly right. Even if you only saw Shantih's eye you knew that she was in a foul mood.

'Such a waste to rub it out,' Jinny thought, testing the page to see if she could pull if free. She loosened the top of the page. 'Might never be able to draw it so well again,' and Jinny's fingers eased a little more of the page away from the book.

'Glory be, Jennifer Manders,' Jinny exclaimed aloud. 'Do you want to be in detention for the rest of this term?' She slammed the French book shut and, bending over her lines, she wrote furiously in wandering columns of words.

'How are you getting on?' Miss Lorimer asked, coming to check.

Jinny uncurled herself and handed the sheets of paper to Miss Lorimer.

'Nearly finished,' she said, hoping Miss Lorimer would let her off with what she had written.

'Might just have time to dash out and see the poster,' Jinny thought as she watched Miss Lorimer push her glasses up her nose and look at Jinny's lines.

Suddenly Miss Lorimer's whole expression changed.

'I suppose this is meant to be a joke?' she demanded, throwing the sheets of paper down in front of Jinny.

Jinny looked at them in amazement, then saw to her horror what had happened. The first twenty three lines read – "I must not deface school property", and then they changed. Over and over again Jinny had written "I must deface school property".

'But I didn't mean . . .'

'Detention tonight,' stated Miss Lorimer. 'Two hundred lines.' She tore the offending sheets of paper into shreds and threw them into the waste-paper basket. 'Start on them now.'

'Is this a record, I ask myself,' Jinny wondered, as she made her way to the detention room. 'Kept in on the first day of term! Something else!'

Jinny pushed the door open. The familiar room was empty. She considered making a dash for it but decided that an hour would make no difference. If the circus was coming tonight she couldn't stop it. The school bus would have gone by now. It was too late to do anything except get on with her lines. With camel-groans of despair Jinny settled herself to write.

Ten minutes later Mr Eccles, Jinny's art master opened the door.

'Jinny!' he exclaimed. 'Don't tell me! Not already! How ever did you manage it?'

Jinny explained.

'Need to get my hands on those books,' said Mr Eccles. 'They'll be worth a fortune in a few years' time.'

Jinny looked dubiously up at him. She felt safer when teachers stayed well on their own side of the fence.

'On you go. I'm meant to be taking detention and I am most certainly not hanging about here watching you write lines, you can do them at home. That writing is excruciating.'

Jinny stuffed paper and pencil into her bag and made for the door.

'Remember, you are not to rub out your drawings. I'll see Miss Lorimer about it.'

Jinny hardly heard him as she ran down the empty

corridor to the cloakroom. She pulled on her jeans, wriggled out of her skirt, hooked it over a peg and, snatching up her coat, pulled it on as she ran across the deserted playground and on through the crowded Inverburgh streets until, gasping for breath, she saw the circus poster ahead of her.

It was the circus that had once owned Shantih. Roberto's Circus. The last time Jinny had seen those words they had been on the sides of the circus vans at the crash. Jinny stared at the poster in a frozen panic. The ringmaster was coming back. Pasted diagonally across the poster – black printing on yellow paper – were the dates of the circus performances.

At first the dates meant nothing to Jinny. Her mind was filled with images of Shantih being taken away from her. Then counting from today, the day she had started school, Jinny realised that it was this week that the circus was coming to Inverburgh. Thursday and Friday. Not tomorrow, but the next day and the next, the circus would be back in Inverburgh. Suddenly Jinny was absolutely certain that the man who had shouted at her from the coach must belong to the circus.

Hardly knowing what she was doing, Jinny spun round and ran full pelt to the bus station. Round and round the bus station she marched, unable to stand or sit. She had to get back to Shantih; had to reach her before the man from the circus tracked her down. If he managed to trace her to Glenbost, which he could do easily, the whole village could tell him where to find a chestnut Arab. Wouldn't need to tell him, for Shantih would be there in the field unguarded. Anyone could steal her.

'I should have jumped off the school bus this morning,' Jinny accused herself, knowing quite well that if she had done so, she would have been knocked down. 'Then I'd have seen the poster and gone straight back to Shantih.'

Plans for hiding in the hills until the circus had gone filled Jinny's head. Her day at school had vanished as if it had never been.

When the bus for Glenbost drew into its bay Jinny pushed her way on to it, hardly giving the passengers time to get off. She banged down into a seat, kicking her heels into the floor in her urgency to be moving. She had to get to Shantih.

Jinny pressed her face against the bus window. There was a bus parked in the next bay. Like the Glenbost bus it had only one passenger – a girl about the same age as Jinny. Unseen Jinny stared at her blankly, thinking only of the threat of the circus.

But gradually, as she gazed, she couldn't help paying attention to the girl on the other bus. She was looking intently at something she was holding in her hands. Her long, straight, black hair was held at the nape of her neck with an elastic band, leaving her pale face exposed and vulnerable. Her lips were pinched tightly together, her chin set, flat cheeks and straight nose seemed clenched into a mask of rigid control. Jinny twisted in her seat, trying to make out what it was that the girl was staring at. It looked like a photograph torn from a magazine but Jinny couldn't quite see the photograph.

As Jinny stretched her neck, peering through the dim glass, the girl started to cry. Tears filled her dark eyes, brimmed over and trickled down her cheeks, but she made no attempt to find a handkerchief or even to wipe her eyes on her coat sleeve. She just sat there crying unlikely tears from the stone mask of her face.

Hot with embarrassment, Jinny looked away quickly.

The bus driver climbed aboard, smiled at Jinny, knowing her well from past detentions. As the bus pulled out of the bay, Jinny couldn't stop herself having a last look at the girl. She was still sitting without moving, her face wet with tears, her strong hands clutching the photograph. But now Jinny could just make out the head of a chunky, bay pony, his bridle emblazoned with a multi-coloured rosette.

At Glenbost Jinny hurtled from the bus, and ran to Shantih's field. Her eyes searched through the gloom for Shantih's chestnut shape. The Arab's welcoming whinny reached Jinny like air to a drowning man. Reaching the field she sprang over the gate, flung her arms round Shantih's neck and buried her face in Shantih's mane.

'They're back,' Jinny told her. 'The circus is back in Inverburgh. I've got to hide you so they can't find you and take you away.'

Jinny's family were totally unaffected by Jinny's news.

'Don't be such a wally,' said Mike. 'Just because the circus is coming to Inverburgh does not mean they are going to try to get Shantih back. Mr MacKenzie bought her from the circus and you bought her from him and that is that.'

'But if the ringmaster offered Mr MacKenzie a lot of money for her he'd say that I hadn't really bought her, only sort of borrowed her,' Jinny insisted. To her panic-stricken mind anything was possible. 'The ringmaster said on the radio that he was going to get her back.'

'Maybe the ringmaster only said he would like to have her back,' suggested Mrs Manders. 'And that is quite a different thing.'

'Listen,' said her father. 'Shantih belongs to you and no one else. That is final.'

'You don't understand,' insisted Jinny, refusing to be reassured. 'I only paid peanuts for her and if that ringmaster wants her back I'm sure he could fix it with Mr MacKenzie.'

'It has nothing to do with Mr MacKenzie,' cried her father.

'Anyway I'm sleeping in the stable in case they try to come and take her away.'

'Who is going to come and take her away?' demanded Mike. 'Who is going to steal her?'

Jinny hardly knew. The only thing she was certain about was that with the circus coming back to Inverburgh, Shantih was in danger.

'I'm not going to school while the circus is here,' she stated.

'Oh Jinny!' despaired her mother. 'You're getting all worked up over nothing. Of course you can't stay off school.'

'I can,' said Jinny, and ignoring her parents' protests she went upstairs to do her homework. On her way up she tracked Ken down in the pottery. He listened attentively to her worries.

'Do you really think they might try to get her back?'

'Of course I do,' declared Jinny. 'That ringmaster was furious at having to leave Shantih behind on the moors. Mr MacKenzie only paid him thirty pounds for her. Think of that, only thirty pounds. I've told you what Mr Simpson's brother heard on the radio. That proves the ringmaster hasn't forgotten about her. I think he'll try to buy her back from Mr MacKenzie and if he offers enough for her, Mr MacKenzie will try to say that he only lent Shantih to me!'

'Straight?' asked Ken. 'You really believe all this?'

'Oh I do! Honestly I do. And if he doesn't manage to buy

her back I think he'll try to steal her. I think he'd stop at nothing to get her back!'

'All illusion,' said Ken. 'Rainbows in the sky. But if you believe it that makes it real for you.'

'It is true.'

'I'll watch her for you then,' Ken promised. 'I'll leave Kelly to guard the field at night and I'll spend Thursday and Friday with the Simpsons. I can watch her from their shop. But your father won't let you stay off school. You'll have to go.'

'S'pose so,' admitted Jinny.

'Circuses!' said Ken in disgust, shuddering. '"By the pricking of my thumbs, something wicked this way comes."'

'Until Saturday,' said Jinny. 'They'll be away by then. Be O.K. once we reach Saturday.'

And at once she thought what a stupid thing she had said; tempting the Gods; challenging them to prove that after Saturday anything could happen. Things so black that they would make the coming of the circus seem like nothing.

That night as Jinny lay in bed, Kelly was in the stables on a warm bed of straw, sleeping with one eye open and both ears alert, knowing that he was there to guard Shantih.

Yet still Jinny lay awake worrying. Suddenly she remembered the girl on the bus and her photograph of the bay pony with his winner's rosette; the unchecked tears trickling down the girl's pale face. And Jinny wondered, with a cold clutch of fate, what black thing had overtaken the girl, to make her sit on the bus, crying openly over a photograph that should have been pinned up proudly on her bedroom wall alongside the brilliant rosette.

CHAPTER THREE

'Could Jennifer Manders come to the headmaster's room, please?'

Hearing her name, Jinny startled awake from her nightmare daydream of Shantih being driven away in a circus van.

'Jinny,' said Mrs Probert, their biology teacher. 'Mr Lawson wants to see you.'

Reluctantly Jinny got to her feet and followed the boy out of the classroom.

'What does he want?' she asked.

'Didn't confide,' said the boy. 'Surprise, surprise.'

'Did he seem furious?'

'Steam from every visisble porthole,' said the boy, leaving Jinny to make her reluctant way to Mr Lawson's room.

'Come in,' called Mr Lawson's deep voice, and Jinny walked into his room to find Miss Lorimer sitting beside him.

'Finished my lines at home,' she thought, her brain computer flashing over why they wanted her. 'Mr Eccles said I wasn't to rub out my drawings. Maybe that's it. Maybe they've sacked him for being on my side and now they want to know what he said to me.'

'Sit down, Jinny,' Mr Lawson said, gesturing to a chair by his desk.

'Now, Miss Lorimer and I want to speak to you about something rather personal. I wouldn't speak to every pupil like this, but I think, and Miss Lorimer agrees with me, that I can trust you. What we're going to tell you is in strictest confidence. No-one but ourselves need know anything about it. Agreed?'

'Affable,' thought Jinny in amazement, nodding her agreement. 'Can't be my drawings.'

'Good. Now, this afternoon a new girl and her mother are coming to see me. Nicola Webster. She had appointments at the Dental Hospital yesterday and this morning so she's starting here tomorrow and she'll be in your class. Until now she has been at Newbury Hall but her parents are getting divorced and she and her mother are living in a flat in Inverburgh. Obviously it will be rather difficult for her leaving a private girls' school and coming here, so we wondered if you would be her friend? Show her round and help her to settle in?'

'But I don't know her,' said Jinny, stating the obvious. 'Maybe she won't want to be friends with me.'

'She has her own pony,' said Miss Lorimer. 'That's why we picked you.'

It was two o'clock when Jinny was again summoned to the headmaster's room. She had spent the day building fantastic dreams around Nicola. Her pony would be a white Arab. She would ride with Jinny at Finmory. Arabs of silver and gold being galloped together over the sands, ridden to the Standing Stones or to Loch Varrich. Or Nicola would be a dressage rider who would be shocked by Jinny's self-taught aids and would instantly set about teaching her the art of dressage. Jinny saw herself walking Shantih into a dressage arena, halting – balanced, correct – touching her stick to the brim of her hat as she saluted the judges, about to ride the winning dressage test.

Or, best of all, Jinny imagined that Nicola would know

some place where she could hide Shantih until the circus had gone.

'You're not so simple as to be taken in by that old chestnut?' Dolina had said when Jinny had told her about Nicola – not about her parents getting divorced but only that she was starting at Inverburgh and, wonder of wonders, had her own pony. 'All he's doing is putting the responsibilities on to you to see if that will calm you down.'

'Don't care,' Jinny had said. 'As long as she rides.'

'Come in,' called Mr Lawson and for the second time that day Jinny opened the headmaster's door and walked into his room.

The woman sitting across the desk from Mr Lawson was hunched into a sheepskin jacket. Her long neck stuck out from its shell, turning a pale face towards Jinny. Her expression twittered nervously about her features.

'Ah, Jinny,' said Mr Lawson, 'this is Mrs Webster.' The woman sprang to her feet, grasping Jinny's hand.

'It's so good of you to offer to look after Nicola. I'm so worried about her. It really is so very kind of you. I just don't know how she'll manage. Such a big change for her.'

Mrs Webster's words poured out in an anxious flood.

'We really are so very grateful.' As suddenly as she had stood up, Mrs Webster collapsed back into her seat again, and for the first time Jinny was able to get a proper look at the girl who was sitting beside her wearing the purple uniform of Newbury Hall.

'She should have changed that,' Jinny thought. 'They'll all make fun of her if she comes here wearing that.'

Then suddenly Jinny realised that there was something familiar about the new girl. She had seen her somewhere before – the pale face with its flat cheekbones, the dark eyes hidden behind metal-rimmed glasses resting on a straight nose and the tufted black hair that looked as if she had cut it herself in a temper.

'Nicola, this is Jinny Manders whom I was telling you about.'

'How do you do?' said Nicola.

'Take Nicola round the school,' Mr Lawson said. 'Give her some idea of the layout of the place, so she won't feel so foreign tomorrow. Come back in about half an hour. Your teacher knows you're showing Nicola round.'

'It's Nick,' said Nicola when the headmaster's door was safely shut behind them. 'He said you've got a pony?'

'Arab,' corrected Jinny.

'Terrific. Lucky you. Have you done much riding? Mine's a show jumper. We've won oodles. He's absolutely brilliant. Only need to enter him and we win. Are you into show jumping, or what?'

'Just riding,' said Jinny edgily. Nick was too much, too sudden, too confident. Even if you'd won the Horse of the Year Show you didn't start boasting about it straight away.

'He's called Brandon. 14.3, bay. Means I have to jump him as a Junior Associate. Suits us. The bigger the jumps the better. Dad didn't really want to buy him when he knew his height. Said I should get a 14·2 but the second I saw Brandon I knew he was the horse to take me to the top. We're going to jump for Britain. That's my ambition, what's yours?'

Still Jinny couldn't think where she had seen Nick before. Couldn't place her and yet she was sure that she had seen her before.

Nick's eyes sparkled behind her glasses. She spoke with breathless enthusiasm, moving at Jinny's side with quick, light steps.

'Listen, do you have to show me round? I mean, after a

morning I'll know it all. Couldn't we nip out for a coke? No one would miss us?'

'We're not allowed . . .' began Jinny.

'Who cares. There must be a cafe nearby. I'll treat you.'

'They'd murder us. Be detention for weeks.'

'So what. Bet you know a way out.'

'You can squeeze through a gap in the wire netting. No one sees you because of the builders' stuff.'

'Right,' said Nick and almost before Jinny had time to realise what was happening, Nick had opened one of the fire doors and they were running across the empty playground.

'Night and darkness,' thought Jinny, visions of years of detention looming before her, as she squeezed through the gap in the netting. 'And I'm supposed to be setting her a good example!'

Running down the side street, Jinny led the way to a café where anyone who could afford it bought chips or ice cream in the lunch hour.

'We'll need to be quick,' Jinny said as they sat down in the furthest corner of the café. She looked round carefully in case there should be any staff sitting at the tables but she didn't see anyone she knew. The café was close to the long distance coach station and was always fairly busy. 'Best not to be too long. Mr Lawson said we'd to be back in half an hour.'

'Don't nag!' said Nicola. 'Can't stand it. You're as bad as Mum. Fuss, fuss, fuss. Drives me bonkers. Lord, I've no cash. Have you any?'

Reluctantly Jinny fished a fifty-pence piece from her pocket. Nick took it and returned with one can of coke and two glasses.

'Tell me about your Arab,' she said. 'What's it called?'

'Shantih.'

'Weird name. Of course Brandon was Brandon when we bought him. Unlucky to change a name. He's registered for show jumping as Brandon of Westwind. That was the name of our house. Mum and I are living in a flat just now. Only temporarily, of course. Dad's down south. Moving south was a big promotion for him. We thought we would have joined him by this time but he's having a bit of bother finding the right house for us. We only had two loose boxes at Westwind so this time he's looking for something with a range of stabling. I want to have several horses.'

'She doesn't know I know her parents are getting divorced,' Jinny thought, listening uneasily to Nick's lies, to her bright voice, to her boasting: wondering how she could tell Nick that she knew her parents were separated.

'I'll want something reliable for the big fences and something fast for speed comps, and I'd like one or two youngsters to be schooling on myself.'

'Really?' said Jinny.

'Oh yes,' said Nick, taking off her glasses and rubbing her eyes. Without her glasses Jinny recognised her at once. She was the girl Jinny had seen on the bus with the long tail of straight black hair that was now cropped into a punk hedgehog. Nick was the girl who had been crying over the photograph of a pony. Jinny could hardly believe that Nick's desolation could have changed into her present embullient confidence. Jinny wondered if the pony in the photograph had been Brandon and what had happened to him to make Nick so miserable.

'I've had other ponies naturally,' continued Nick. 'But Brandon was my first real show jumper. He's not much to look at, bit cobby, but can he jump! Once at home he cleared six feet.'

'And some,' thought Jinny.

'It's not only the height he can clear, he's got brains too. If he's wrong-strided he can sort himself out. Mind you, it's me as well. He knows I'm not going to yank him in the mouth or come crashing down on his loins. I don't know why some horses go on jumping, the things their riders do to them to stop them jumping.'

From the opposite corner of the café a young man who had been watching the two girls, stood up and started to move across towards them. He had bright blue eyes, light hair and was wearing cords and a quilted jacket.

'Excuse me,' he said. 'Aren't you the girl I saw riding a chestnut Arab?'

Jinny stared blankly up at him, her heart battering in her throat.

'What?' she said. 'What do you mean?'

'I saw you the other day, riding on the road to Inverburgh. I was on a coach. You must have seen me shouting to you.'

'I don't know what you're talking about,' denied Jinny.

'But you've got an . . .' began Nick before her sentence ended in a yelp of pain as Jinny kicked her hard on the leg.

'We've got to get back,' stated Jinny, jumping to her feet, pushing past the young man.

'Here wait a minute! It *was* you. I'd know that red hair anywhere.'

With Nick close behind her, Jinny bolted from the café. The second they were outside Jinny grabbed Nick's arm and dragged her into the opening at the side of the café. Crouching behind piles of litter-filled cardboard boxes they saw the man run past.

'Quick,' mouthed Jinny. 'This way,' and running down the close she sprang up on to dustbins, leapt over a wall and dropped down into a garden on the other side of the wall. A spaniel at a window exploded into a fury of barking as the trespassers ran out of his garden.

'Can't tell you now,' said Jinny. 'Got to get back to school.' She raced on down the side street. At the corner she stopped and peered out into the main road. The young man was walking towards them.

'He's there,' Jinny gasped, and grabbing Nick she forced her into a doorway.

Peering out they saw the man pass, hesitate, then walk quickly on.

'Back the way we came,' ordered Jinny and they raced back, cut through a side entrance and dodged round side streets until they reached the gap in the school's boundary netting.

'What was all that about?' demanded Nick.

'He's from the circus,' gasped Jinny. 'The circus Shantih used to belong to. I'm sure they're trying to get her back.'

As Jinny spoke, Mr Lawson, with Nick's mother, crouched in her caddis shell of sheepskin, appeared at the school door.

'Ah, girls,' said Mr Lawson. 'We've been looking for you. Showing Nicola our playing fields?'

'I'm really keen on hockey,' said Nick, her face bright with honest enthusiasm. 'I was in the hockey team at Newbury Hall, that's why I asked Jinny to let me see the pitch.'

'She can't half lie,' thought Jinny with grudging admiration.

'Yes,' said Mr Lawson. 'We're very proud of our new sports facilities. I'm sure Mrs McPhee will be only too pleased to make use of your prowess at hockey.'

'Super,' said Nick, beaming.

'Now, we'll see you tomorrow morning, Nicola. Your mother has explained the circumstances to me and there is no need for you to buy a new uniform. I quite understand.'

Jinny saw Nick look at her, quick, calculating, but Jinny was too worried about Shantih to care what Nicola wore. She could have come to school in a nightdress for all Jinny cared.

'And Mrs Webster, any time I can be of any assistance, don't hesitate to get in touch.'

Mrs Webster twisted her lips together. 'So very kind of you,' she said, her eyes filling with tears. 'So very kind.'

Mr Lawson walked with Jinny to her classroom otherwise she would have gone straight home to Shantih. Instead, she had to sit through two periods of Science staring at the classroom door, expecting it to open and Mr Lawson to come in with the young man, to see if he could identify the girl he was looking for. Then there was the slowness of the bus to be endured before she saw Shantih and Bramble grazing securely in their field.

'Of course he's from the circus,' Jinny said, riding home with Mike. 'The circus comes on Thursday and he's come on ahead. Must have been told to keep a lookout for Shantih and now he's found her.'

'Might be someone from T.V. or a publisher looking for a chestnut Arab to photograph. You're probably running away from Shantih's big chance.'

'That will be right,' said Jinny.

'You'll be for the circus, then?' asked Mr MacKenzie as they rode past the farmyard. 'You'll be taking Shantih along just to be giving her a wee reminder of the good old days?'

Jinny looked down at the old farmer. He was buttoned securely into tweed jacket, waistcoat and trousers. The ends of his trousers were joined to his hobnail boots by buckled gaiters. A tweed cap was pulled down over his brows and in its shadow his eyes darted to and fro, missing nothing. A black, short-stemmed pipe was held between the gaps in his yellow teeth.

Unable to stop herself, Jinny said, 'If that ringmaster came here trying to get Shantih back, you'd tell him that she's mine now? Nothing to do with you anymore. You would, wouldn't you?'

Mr MacKenzie's eyes glinted. He took the pipe from his mouth and spat thoughtfully.

'Now that is the wee problem you have put to me, and the answer would be depending on how much that same man was holding out in his hand. If it was the thousands he had in it I'm thinking I might be mentioning to your father the food she has had stuffed into her and him not paying for the half of it. There is many would be on my side in thinking I had the right to her.'

'Of course he was only teasing you,' said Mike as they rode on. 'Go asking him that kind of question and you're just encouraging him to have you on. He can't sell Shantih. She belongs to you. Anyway I've heard him boasting to people about how well you ride. He likes you.'

'Wouldn't make any difference. If he wanted to get her back he would.'

'O.K., O.K.,' said Mike, abandoning his sister to her certainties. 'Have it the way you want it.'

'I'll be straight back,' Jinny told Shantih as she turned her loose. 'I'll make a sandwich of my dinner and bring it down here. Do my homework in the stable.'

But Shantih wasn't listening. Her forelegs folded, she stretched out her neck, kicked herself off and rolled, scrubbing herself into the deliciously muddy ground. No memories of circus lights or of the ringmaster's whip would trouble her grazing, but to Jinny running back to the house, every clump of rhododendrons shielded the crouching figure of the young man from the circus who had tracked her down.

'I hope,' said Mrs Manders, setting a plate of broth in front of Jinny, 'that this isn't going to turn into a nonsense.'

Jinny slurped down the hot soup.

'I must stay with her,' she insisted. 'I can't go to school.'

'Don't start,' warned her father. 'We've all told you there is no chance of the circus coming for Shantih. She belongs to you. Now stop it.'

Jinny put her elbows on the table, buried her head in her hands, tears welled in her eyes. It was no good. They would never believe her until it was too late.

When Jinny had learnt her french vocabulary, fought her way through an arithmetic exercise and read a chapter of history she went out to the field.

'Half an hour,' her mother called after her.

'Yes,' said Jinny defeated.

The night was clear and cold, a first touch of frost sparkling the stars. Ken and Kelly were waiting by the field gate, watching Shantih's elegant grace and Bramble's bulk grazing together.

'No-one ever listens to me,' said Jinny, leaning over the top of the gate and calling to Shantih for the joy of feeling her delicate lipping against her open palm. 'The circus will be in Inverburgh tomorrow and nobody cares.'

'I've told you I'll watch her. Kelly is guarding the field at night. She is safe. Why did you run away from the man? Why didn't you wait to find out what he wanted?'

'Because I know they're planning to get Shantih.'

'No use anyone telling you otherwise then,' said Ken. 'Not if you know.'

Shantih came slowly towards them, her eyes were liquid, moon-bright; her pricked ears, dark triangles above the silken fall of her forelock. She breathed grass-sweet breath over Jinny and rested her head on Jinny's shoulder.

'I just love her so much,' said Jinny, her face against Shantih's silken neck. 'So much I can't bear to think of anything happening to her.'

'Love her too much,' said Ken. 'It's not only the circus. It will be away by next week but you'll still be worrying.'

CHAPTER FOUR

'We won our first really big class at Hazelrigg. That was one thing about Newbury Hall, they were very decent about letting you do your own thing. Didn't mind a bit when I took days off for shows. We'd gone down to Hazelrigg with Aunt Ag and when I saw the course I just knew Brandon was going to love it. Really huge spreads.'

Jinny munched baked beans on toast, chewing noisily inside her head, doing her best to block off the incessant sound of Nick's voice. It was Friday lunchtime and the two girls were sitting in the school dining hall.

On Thursday morning, from the school bus, Jinny had seen men setting up the big top so she knew the circus had arrived. When she had got home that evening Ken had been waiting at Glenbost.

'Not even a clown,' he had reported.

'Shan't be safe until Saturday,' Jinny had said. 'But thanks for watching.'

'Safe now,' insisted Ken.

'I should be with her,' Jinny thought wretchedly. 'Not sitting here listening to Nick. Bet she doesn't even remember Shantih's name and I know utter everything about her bloomin' Brandon.'

'Richard, he's my cousin – Aunt Ag's son . . .'

'I know! I know!' Jinny screamed under her breath. Nick's Aunt Agnes and her three children had featured largely in all Nick's stories. They lived at Foxholm, a few miles on the other side of Inverburgh, in a house which, according to Nick, was more or less a mansion. Aunt Ag kept horses at livery, schooled difficult horses and gave private lessons. The oldest cousin – Linda – was at university, Richard, who was seventeen, helped Aunt Ag in the stables and Stephanie, known as Steph, was eight. They all rode and show jumped and had all been more or less born in the saddle while Aunt Ag was showing her hunters.

'You'd like Aunt Ag,' Nick had assured Jinny. 'She just lives for horses. Nothing is too much trouble for her, if it's to do with horses. She'll do anything to help you. Look at the way they're keeping Brandon for me. Where would we be without her? But I do wish Dad would get a move on and find a house for us. I can't bear not being able to ride Brandon.'

'But you can ride at the weekends, can't you?'

'Not this weekend. In fact not,' Nick had said. 'It's so difficult to get to Foxholm. No through bus. Mum doesn't like me going by myself and of course while Dad's away we don't have a car.'

'Can't Aunt Ag come and pick you up?' Jinny had demanded, beginning to doubt even Aunt Ag's existence.

'Actually, no. She's away this weekend. I'm going to be so bored shut up in that pokey little flat. I was wondering if I could visit you. How far is it to Finmory?'

'Miles,' said Jinny, squashing Nick's obvious wish for an invitation. 'Miles and miles. You couldn't think of coming to see me. If Foxholm is too far, Finmory is off the globe.'

'We could have gone for a ride,' Nick had suggested but Jinny had ignored her.

Since Nick had started at Inverburgh Comprehensive she had made no attempt to speak to any of the other children. She spoke only to Jinny, telling her in endless detail how well Brandon had performed at every show he had been to. She took no interest in Shantih and even when Jinny had explained about the circus Nick had said, 'But she belongs to you,' and gone back to Brandon.

'When I was walking the course at Blandyke I noticed Prue Campbell pacing out the distance between the brush fence and the wall. She did it three times so I figured there must be something odd about it. I went back and paced it out again myself and she was right. If I'd let Brandon gallop on at the brush he'd have been through the wall.'

Jinny finished her baked beans.

'But when it came to the jump-off there was only Prue Campbell and myself in it. She went first and was clear so I just had to risk it. Brandon knew he was coming wrong at the wall, he went right in, far too close, or so I thought, then he literally took off straight into the air and cleared it, so we won.'

'If we don't go now we're going to be late for English.'

Still talking, Nick walked at Jinny's side.

'I remember at Broughton Show there was this post and rails and you just had to come in at it from an angle . . .'

'Shut up,' Jinny mouthed silently. 'Shut up, shut up.'

She stared with open dislike at Nick's pale face, her tufted black hair and her glittering spectacles. It didn't seem to make any difference how much Jinny ignored her and tried to change the subject, Nick just went on talking about Brandon.

'She's making it all up,' Jinny decided. 'Don't believe any of it. It's all lies, like her father looking for a house for them. Probably hasn't even got a pony. That's why she wants to come to Finmory, so she can ride Shantih. Well, I'm not asking her.'

'Of course that's what makes Brandon so special. He

uses his brains, looks for the shortest way round. Sometimes I think he knows the course as well as I do.'

But much as Jinny was irritated by Nick she couldn't, not a hundred percent hate her. Not when she had met her anxious, face-changing, pathetic mother; not when she knew her parents were separated; not when she had watched her crying on the bus.

'Wish I'd never seen her,' thought Jinny. 'Wish Mr Lawson hadn't picked on me to look after her.'

At a quarter to four Miss Lorimer came into their French class. She apologised to Mrs Carr for interrupting her lesson, then asked Nick if she had been given all her textbooks.

'Not any,' said Nick.

'I'm going to the book store now. You've just got time to come with me and I'll look out a set of second-year books for you. Jinny, you can come too and help us to carry them, that is if Mrs Carr will excuse you both.'

'I mustn't miss the school bus,' said Jinny sourly, clutching up her school bag, but Miss Lorimer paid no attention to her.

They were still in the book store when the four o'clock bell blasted through the school.

'I'll need to dash,' said Jinny, looking for somewhere to dump the armful of books which Miss Lorimer had handed to her.

'Only one more Biology book,' Miss Lorimer said to Nick, checking her list, 'and that's your full set.'

Jinny put her books on the floor.

'Not there, bring them to my room,' fussed Miss Lorimer.

'The bus won't wait,' exclaimed Jinny.

'Of course it will. Won't take you a second to bring them along to my room. Now, where did I put my glasses?'

Nick handed them to her.

'Yes, now,' said Miss Lorimer. 'One last check to make quite sure you have everything.'

It took five minutes and by the time Jinny went charging across the playground, all the buses had gone.

'Miss Lorimer did it on purpose,' stormed Jinny. 'She knows there's not another bus until six. Might just as well have sent me to detention,' and she stood in the pouring rain, scowling back at the school.

Nick came out of the school door, dwarfed by the emptiness of the deserted playground, she walked towards Jinny.

'Has it gone?' she asked.

'What does it bloomin' look like,' snapped Jinny.

'Shall we go and have a coke?' Nick offered.

'No money,' said Jinny.

'Nor me,' said Nick.

'But we could go to your flat. It's near the bus station and better than standing here in the pouring rain.'

'Not terribly convenient,' said Nick. 'Mum's out at work. I was meant to tidy up before I came to school but I didn't have time.'

'As if I'd care. I only want to wait until it's time for my bus.'

Nick hesitated as if she were trying to find another excuse to stop her having to ask Jinny into their flat.

'It's pouring,' stated Jinny. 'Come on or we'll be drowned.' She set off decidedly in the direction of Nick's flat.

The flat was one of a block of modern flats built a few years ago. Surrounded by Inverburgh's gaunt tenements they looked like a pile of children's building blocks left out by mistake.

'We're only here for a week or two,' Nick protested as the inside stair climbed upward between graffiti-scrawled walls. 'It was all so sudden. Mum and I had to get somewhere at once. I'll let you see some photographs of Westwind. It was not in the least like this.'

And Jinny wondered if it had been sudden – Mr Webster expected home for an ordinary meal at the end of an ordinary day, then coming in and announcing that he was leaving them. Or had Nick known that things were going wrong in her parents' marriage – Jinny imagined the weeks of listening, straining to hear conversations in hushed voices, waking at night to hear your parents fighting and worst of all, the days when your parents seemed to be happy with each other and you would pray that they weren't going to split up after all, that it wasn't going to happen. Jinny wondered what they had actually said to Nick and how she had found words to cover her heartbreak. Probably she would never know. Nick had told so many lies about the house her father was going to buy for them in England, that Jinny just hadn't been able to tell her that she knew the truth about her parents.

Nick took a key from her school bag and opened the pale blue door. The hall was so small that Jinny and Nick were squashed together as they took off their wet clothes and hung them from plastic pegs stuck to the wall. Three doors opened from the hall – a bathroom where Jinny glimpsed a stained bath and mini washbasin, a bedroom door only just ajar and the door Nick opened into the living room.

'Would you like a cup of tea? I'm pretty useless at this sort of thing but I can just about cope with tea bags.'

Jinny stood staring about her. It was like being inside a cardboard box, low-ceilinged and with walls that you knew were flimsy even when you hadn't touched them.

At one end of the room was a bed settee, the bedclothes trailing to the floor. At the other end a cooker, sink and kitchen cupboard crouched together behind a perspex screen. There were two shabby, easy chairs, a small, plastic-topped table and two wooden chairs. By each chair the cheap carpet was worn away by the feet of the people who had perched here. Really it was all right, brilliant compared to some of the rooms Jinny had visited with her father in Stopton, but Jinny couldn't stop herself wondering what it must be like to have to spend your evenings and weekends shut into this tiny room with Mrs Webster's twisting face sitting opposite you.

'This isn't our stuff,' said Nick, appearing from behind the screen with two steaming mugs of tea. 'We had to put all our stuff into store. We were jolly lucky to have found this place. But it is so mini. That's why Mum goes out to work at the advertising agency. She used to be a copywriter and they were delighted to have her back. She said she'd die of claustrophobia shut up in here all day. Let's take this through to my room and I'll show you some photos of Brandon.'

If the living room was small, Nick's bedroom was a cupboard, but its walls were encrusted with photographs, all of Nick, riding, jumping, leading, grooming, the same bay pony.

'That's Brandon.' The pony's name caught in Nick's throat, hard to say.

Jinny looked closely at the photographs. The dark bay pony had a thick, black mane and tail, four black stockings and neat ebony hooves. His back was too short, his neck too thick and his head with its black muzzle was as chunky as if it had been chiselled out of wood and newly varnished. He had small, bright eyes, quizzing the camera, and in nearly all the photographs his rather large ears were pricked sharply forward. Out of all the horses or ponies Jinny had seen, Brandon was the only one who looked as if he had a sense of humour.

'He's super,' Jinny exclaimed.

'That's my favourite,' said Nick and pointed to one where the camera had caught Brandon at the height of his leap. There was the red and white show jump, a space of blue sky and looking as if he was hanging in the air, high above the jump, was Brandon. His legs were tucked tightly to his body, his head turned, as if, in mid-air, he was spying out the next jump. Sitting well forward was Nick, her hair in two long plaits, flying behind her and her face under her hard hat lit up with joy.

'That was at Stanley,' said Nick. 'And that was the rosette we won.' She pointed one out from about four dozen that were arranged on the wall at the foot of her bed.

Somehow, now that she was in her own room, surrounded by photographs of Brandon, Nick had stopped irritating Jinny. It was fascinating to hear how she had won the different rosettes and what the judges had said to her at different shows.

'That's Westwind, taken not this summer but the one before.'

Westwind was a snow-cemmed, detached house. Standing on the gravel path leading to the sun porch was Nick, holding Brandon. Beside her, a tall man in jeans and an open-necked shirt had one arm round Nick's shoulders and the other arm round Mrs Webster's waist. They were all smiling. The garden stretched about them in immaculate lawns, a horse chestnut tree and brilliant flowerbeds.

'Is that your father?' Jinny asked and her voice sounded like Petra's.

Nick glanced, quick and sharp, at her. 'Yes,' she said and drew Jinny's attention to another photograph.

It was only a quarter past five when Nick suggested that it was time for Jinny to leave.

'Be O.K. if I wait until half-past.'

'You don't want to miss this bus too,' Nick insisted. 'I'll walk down with you.'

'There will be nothing to do except hang around until the bus arrives. We'll be far too early.'

'Better too early than too late,' said Nick, fetching Jinny's coat.

Jinny took it reluctantly. She hated having to hang around the bus station, trying to avoid the Inverburgh drunks who always seemed to pick on her for their meth-smelling confidences. She would far rather have gone on looking at Brandon's photographs.

'Left my bag in the other room,' Jinny said, and went to get it, while Nick waited impatiently at the outside door, her hand on the doorknob.

'Wants rid of me,' Jinny thought, feeling Nick's barely-concealed impatience hurrying her out.

Jinny had just picked up her school bag when she heard someone coming in.

'Mum!' exclaimed Nick. 'You're early. Jinny's here. We're dashing for her bus. Got to rush or we'll miss it.'

'Jinny, how nice to see you again. Such a night.' Mrs Webster, her sodden sheepskin dripping about her, came into the room.

'Right, we're away,' Nick shouted.

Mrs Webster laid a restraining hand on Jinny's arm.

'Now, now, don't be rushing off before I've thanked you. So kind of your parents to invite Nick for the weekend. I do so appreciate it. She'd have been alone here all weekend.

Refuses to go to her Aunt Ag's and I'll be out at work, so I can't tell you how pleased I am that she's spending the weekend with you.'

Jinny stared in blank amazement at Mrs Webster while Mrs Webster stared back, her mouth pinned in its frozen smile, her eyes knowing that something had gone wrong.

'But I never . . .' began Jinny, then stopped herself. Clear in her memory was the thought of Nick crying on the bus; the picture of the Websters and Brandon safe in the summer sunshine of last year. What would she feel like if she were Nick?

'Yes, um. Well, goodbye.' said Jinny and followed Nick out of the flat.

'Well?' she demanded when they were both outside. 'What did your mother mean? Did you tell her that I'd asked you to Finmory?'

'She's got it all mixed up. I only said I might go and see you.'

'Suppose you said you might stay for the weekend too?'

'She gets muddled.'

'Huh! I bet,' Jinny snorted. 'Someone's muddled, that's for sure.'

They walked to the bus station in silence. The last thing Jinny wanted was to have to listen to Nick boasting about Brandon all weekend. She didn't want her. Did not want her at all. She wanted to spend the weekend with Shantih. To know that the circus had gone and Shantih was out of danger.

They stopped when they reached the bus station and stood for a minute, still not speaking.

'Well . . .' said Nick.

'Don't do it,' Jinny warned herself. 'Don't say it. You do not want her.' Then she heard herself saying, as she had known she would – 'If you really want to come, I suppose you can.'

'D'you mean it?' Nick, turned the blaze of her round-lensed glasses straight on Jinny. 'Of course I really want to come, course I do. Who'd want to be stuck in that beastly little flat all weekend?'

'Well come then,' said Jinny groaning in her depths. 'Tomorrow morning. There's a bus leaves here at nine. I'll meet you in Glenbost. You can ride Bramble,' and with a touch of joy Jinny realised that when she saw Nick in Glenbost it would be Saturday – the day the circus left Inverburgh.

'Oh super to be riding again. Thank you. I'll be on the bus. See you then.' Nick turned away, a lightness in her step that hadn't been there before.

'And next weekend perhaps we can go to your Aunt Ag's and ride Brandon.'

At the sound of Jinny's voice, Nick had paused, looked over her shoulder. As she heard what Jinny was saying her expression changed into the blank despair that Jinny had first seen from the bus.

CHAPTER FIVE

Sitting astride Shantih and holding Bramble's reins, Jinny waited for the bus to arrive from Inverburgh.

'Give over,' she said sharply as Bramble glowered, reached out his neck and snapped at Shantih's withers. 'I know it's Saturday and you shouldn't be here but that's life. Never know when it's going to put the boot in. And today is one of your boot days, so you may as well make the most of it.'

Bramble regarded Jinny with a calculating eye. He was not one to make the best of a bad job. When Bramble sulked he was not to be moved.

Jinny's mouth twisted up at the corners. No matter how many rosettes Nick had won for show jumping she would meet her match in Bramble when he was sulking.

The bus rattled into Glenbost, stopped, and Nick was the first to get off. Mrs Simpson's sister and her little girl got off next and third was a young man with light brown hair. Jinny froze. For a split second of paralysing fear she was certain he was the man from the coach, from the circus. Then she saw him more clearly and recognised him as Andy Price from a farm at Ardtallon.

'Hi,' shouted Nick. 'Smashing day. I got it all sorted out with Mum. I'd said to her that I'd like to come for the weekend and she thought I'd said I *was* coming. That's how we got mixed up.'

'Was it,' said Jinny, accepting the speech Nick had obviously been rehearsing on the bus.

'The circus haven't scrobbled her yet?'

'No.'

Now that it was Saturday and the circus due to leave Inverburgh today, Jinny was beginning to see her family's point of view. Although Ken had watched Mrs Simpson's field all day Friday, there had been no sign of anyone from the circus. Maybe it had all been her imagination. Maybe when she had bought Shantih from Mr MacKenzie that did make Shantih her own horse for always.

'Utterly mine,' thought Jinny, clapping Shantih's sleek neck.

'No one can take you away from me.' Yet the vivid memory of how keen the young man had been to find out about Shantih still haunted her.

'Golden Arab,' said Nick, holding out her hand to Shantih. 'She is a real Arab, isn't she? Can she jump? Not many pure-bred Arabs can.'

'Oh, she can jump. She's won a cup.'

'Where?' Nick's question was dagger-sharp.

'Inverburgh Show.'

'Oh that,' said Nick. 'More farmers and sheep than horses. Not much competition there. I never bother taking Brandon to it.'

Jinny wanted to tell her that the year Shantih had won there had been competition. There had been Claire Burnley with her top show jumper from England.

'Could I have a jump on her?' Nick asked before Jinny had time to speak.

'No, sorry, I never let anyone else ride Shantih. I've brought Bramble for you. If you want to jump we can ride up the moors from here. I've marked the walls with whitewash, so we can gallop on, jumping when we come to them.'

'O.K.,' agreed Nick, taking Bramble's reins, speaking to him. 'Looks a bit of a character this one.'

Jinny watched her tighten Bramble's girths and mount.

'You know he'll stop with her,' said the voice in Jinny's head. 'Even if she gets him to canter without being bucked off, he'll drop his shoulder or stop dead at a wall. Don't be so rotten, warn her,' but the echo of Nick's boasting rang in Jinny's mind and she said nothing.

Shantih strode out in a flowing walk. Looking urgently forward, the fine strands of her forelock mazed around her face. She knew that coming on to the moors from the village meant jumping. Jinny glanced over her shoulder, expecting to see Bramble crabbing along but he wasn't. He was close behind Shantih, striding out with a surprised expression on his face.

'Won't be that when we start to jump,' Jinny told herself. She didn't want Bramble to go well for Nick. She wanted Nick to have a struggle to manage him; she wanted Bramble to put in one of his full gallop to instant, head-down stops and send Nick shooting into the bracken.

'Not hurt herself,' Jinny thought. 'Just come off.'

'There's the first wall,' Jinny shouted, pointing. 'Keep Bramble behind me. Jump where I jump.'

'Will do.'

'Just watch he doesn't stop,' Jinny added, relenting.

'He won't stop with me,' Nick said, her pale face flushed with delight at the prospect of jumping. 'You don't need to worry about me.'

Jinny released her fingers on Shantih's reins. The Arab broke into a trot and Jinny touched her into a canter. The splash of white on the dry stone wall drew Shantih to it like a magnet. Jinny gathered her together and sitting down in her saddle she rode her at the wall. Shantih leapt, soared and touched down. Jinny twisted round to see Bramble pounding at the wall.

'He'll stop,' Jinny thought with guilty delight. 'That's what Bramble likes, flat out and then wham!'

But Bramble didn't stop. He bustled over the wall without any hesitation.

'Huh!' thought Jinny and she rode Shantih on to the next wall.

She jumped the next three walls without looking back, knowing only from the beat of Bramble's following hooves that Nick was still in control.

As Jinny cantered in a wide sweep to the next jump, a wall with a burn running on the far side of it, Nick urged Bramble up beside Shantih.

'Jump it as a pair,' she challenged.

'No,' Jinny yelled back. 'You can only jump where I've painted it.'

'Rubbish! Jump these doddy little walls anywhere.'

Jinny wanted to tell her that jumping walls on the moors wasn't like show jumping with flat take-offs and clear landings. Sheep climbing the walls knocked stones to the ground: heather and bracken trapped unwary hooves and rabbit burrows could send even the cleverest horse crashing to the ground.

'You're not scared, are you?'

'It's sense,' said Jinny. 'Nothing to do with being scared.' But Nick's words taunted her. She rode Shantih at the wall and Bramble kept pace beside her. Highland pony and Arab rose together, cleared the wall and landed together.

'S'easy,' said Nick.

For the next three walls Nick rode at her side and nothing Jinny could do would shake her off.

She thought of telling her that it wasn't good for Bramble

being made to gallop like that but it was obvious that Bramble was thoroughly enjoying himself. He seemed to have grown to at least sixteen hands. His neck was crested, his nostrils blood-red pits, his eyes sparkled with excitement and his hooves pranced from the ground as he searched eagerly for the next jump. Jinny had never seen him like this before. She had never known that he could jump like this.

'She's showing off,' Jinny thought. 'Getting him all worked up. What does she think she's doing, upsetting him like that. Making me invite her and then showing off.'

'That's enough,' Jinny announced, scowling. 'They're only out at grass. Not your fancy show jumpers.'

'They're both as fit as fleas,' Nick said. 'You don't think I'd gallop a horse that wasn't fit, do you?'

Jinny thought she would do anything to be able to show off. She steadied Shantih to a walk.

'Anyway, that's enough,' she said.

'I jumped Brandon on the moors round Aunt Ag's once. Richard was on Warrior. We just went charging round. One gate had wire above it and we didn't even stop for that. Over hunt jumps, the lot. I quite enjoy this kind of thing now and again but I'm not really interested in it. Show jumping makes bouncing over little walls seem pretty boring. Did I tell you Brandon jumped six feet once?'

'You did,' stated Jinny. 'I haven't known you for a week and you have mentioned it several times.'

'Yes, well, it is pretty good for a 14·3 horse. As I said, it makes these little walls seem nothing.'

Jinny thought of the drop jump. If she didn't tell Nick it was a drop she would come off there all right. No one could stay on Bramble over that, if they didn't know it was a drop.

'This way,' said Jinny, turning Shantih towards the Finmory moors.

When they were close to the wall with the drop Jinny asked Nick if she wanted to jump a few more walls.

'Course,' said Nick at once.

'That one,' said Jinny pointing. 'Then that one. Jump it this side of the hawthorn. And then that one.'

Almost, almost Jinny added, 'Look out for the last. There's a huge drop on the other side,' but she didn't. She thought hard about how well Bramble was jumping for Nick, and said nothing.

'This time keep behind me. If you jump in the wrong place you could land on boulders or straight into a boggy bit.'

'Yes, Miss Manders,' mocked Nick.

'That's it. Serve her right,' thought Jinny, and collecting Shantih rode her at the first wall.

Jinny picked a place at the second wall where fallen stones turned it into a spread, knowing that this would make Nick more careful when she approached the drop.

Shantih flew the spread, landing far out beyond the scattering of stones and Jinny steadied her for the downhill canter to the drop wall.

'Ride her at it,' Jinny told herself. 'Ride as if it were an ordinary wall.'

But Jinny felt her stomach clench, her mouth go suddenly brick-dry. There was nothing in her mind now but the thought of the drop – the threat of the circus, Nick's maddening superiority – had all vanished. There was only the tight anticipation of the falling into nothingness which Jinny dreaded.

The wall rushing at her, Jinny shouted aloud to encourage herself. Feeling Shantih lift, she sat back automatically, letting her reins slip through her fingers to the buckle, and endured the interminable seconds of the fall into space. Still on automatic pilot, she felt Shantih land safely and canter on downhill. It was over. She had survived.

Coming back into herself Jinny gathered up her reins and twisted round to see Bramble's head appear over the top of the wall. For seconds he seemed to balance there, poised to jump and then he launched himself into a clumsy, unwilling leap. Sitting forward over Bramble's almost nonexistent withers, Nick never moved in the saddle. The instant Bramble pounded to earth she was in control again.

'And shucks to you, Jennifer Manders,' Jinny said to herself.

'Right,' she said aloud. 'Better get home now or we'll be late for lunch.'

'You knew there was a drop, didn't you?' demanded Nick as she walked Bramble at Shantih's side. She wasn't annoyed or resentful but laughing; seeing it without fear, only as a good joke.

'There is a bit of a drop,' admitted Jinny.

'Nothing compared to the slide at Hickstead,' said Nick in the tone of voice that made Jinny think she must have jumped over the Hickstead course scores of times.

Riding up the lane from Mr MacKenzie's farm, Nick saw the field where Jinny had her jumps.

'Are those yours?' she cried, standing up in her stirrups to see them better.

'Bit of a mess now,' said Jinny, regarding the rusty cans, the mouldering straw bales, rubber tyres and the assortment of poles covered in flaking red and white paint, which made up her jumps.

'Could we jump this afternoon?'

'They've done enough this morning,' said Jinny quickly.

'Oh, I don't mean a jumping session. I'd just like to try

Bramble over a decent-sized jump. He's got some pop in him for a Highland and I'd love to see you jump Shantih. Let's feed them and leave them in for an hour or two, then have a jump. Honestly it wouldn't do them any harm.'

'Well . . .' said Jinny reluctantly.

'Go on,' persuaded Nick. 'I really would love to see Shantih jumping.'

When Shantih and Bramble had been watered, fed and were munching down their hay, Jinny went up to the house and returned with a flask of soup, egg rolls and chocolate biscuits.

'They all say it's very rude of me and you'll be shocked at my disgusting manners but I don't care,' she said as she poured the soup into mugs. 'If you want you can go in and meet them, but I have to stay with Shantih until the circus has gone. It's billed to be in Bridge of Marr tonight but until I know it's away I have to stay with Shantih.'

'You could leave her now,' said Nick.

'There you are, you're exactly the same as the rest of them. You don't believe that the ringmaster is trying to get her back. You think I'm making a fuss about nothing.'

'If he had been interested in buying her back he'd have been at the house before now. But I'm telling you it's O.K. to leave her now,' insisted Nick, laughing at Jinny.

'I suppose you think that's funny? Think it's a joke that they might take Shantih away from me? Well if that's the sort of thing that amuses you it does not amuse me.'

'Actually I don't find it at all funny.' Nick's voice was suddenly dry and hard. 'All I'm doing is trying to tell you that the circus has left. My bus was held up by the circus vans this morning. So Shantih's safe.'

'Gone?' Jinny gasped. 'Truly? You're not just kidding me?'

'Honest.'

Jinny leapt up from the straw bales where she had been sitting, flipped into a cartwheel of delight, then ran to Shantih.

'They've gone,' she yelled. 'They're away and they haven't got you.' She flung her arms round Shantih's neck.

'You're safe,' she whispered, her face buried into the strong, good-smelling bulk of her horse. 'Dear, dear Shantih. No one can take you away from me now. Horse come-to-stay for always.'

Jinny stood back from Shantih, holding in her mind's eye every detail of her Arab mare – the tucked corners of her lips, the fluted curve of her nostrils, her arched neck, the clear lines of her body and straight, iron-strong legs. She was so beautiful.

'Must let Ken know,' Jinny shouted and went running up to the house her long hair bannering behind her. 'The circus has gone,' she shouted. 'They've left. Nick saw them going.'

Each member of her family, in their own way, said they had told her so, and that if Jinny had listened to them she would have saved herself a lot of worry.

'She enjoys it,' condescended Petra. 'Always creating about nothing.'

'Listen who's talking,' said Jinny, hurrying out of the kitchen in search of Ken.

'Fine,' said Ken when Jinny told him and thanked him for guarding Shantih. 'That's good.' His slow smile lit up the sea green flecks in his eyes. His long-fingered hands shaped the clay on the wheel into melting, shifting shapes.

'Be glad,' insisted Jinny. 'Be really pleased.'

'Things happen both good and bad,' said Ken, unmoved.

'Well I'm delirious. All joyful. Filled with such delight.'

'Did you really think the ringmaster could take her from you?'

'Yes.'

'Our thoughts make things happen, bring them to us.'

'Got to get back to Nick,' said Jinny, escaping from Ken.

Sitting on the tack room table, swinging her legs, Jinny was lost in a glow of contentment. Nick's show jumping stories were no longer boring but fascinating, and when they eventually went down to Mr MacKenzie's field to jump, Jinny felt nothing but admiration for Nick's riding.

Riding, quietly, neatly, it was no time until Nick had Bramble paying attention to her. With hardly visible aids she sent Bramble trotting and cantering round the field. When she began to jump him, Bramble stood back from the jumps, clearing them in wide arcs, with none of his usual stubborn cat jumps.

'You next,' said Nick. Shantih, who had been plunging and fretting as she waited for her turn, roared forward.

Jinny had no intention of checking her. She wanted her to fly the jumps, to gallop and soar. They went round the six ramshackle jumps twice, then it took Jinny several rounds of the field to bring Shantih back under control again.

'The exception!' cried Nick. 'An Arab who can jump! What height has she cleared?'

'Dunno,' said Jinny, not caring. She thought it likely that Shantih could jump ten feet; could jump the moon; now that the circus had gone. They rode back by Finmory Bay, leaving furrows of hoof prints in the sands. Jinny's world lapped her round with peace.

Later when they had turned Bramble and Shantih out, Jinny waited, leaning over the gate, wanting nothing more than to go on gazing at her beloved horse. Nick stood a little way off, not looking at the horses, not speaking, drawn into herself. Gradually her withdrawn silence reached Jinny.

'Sorry,' she exclaimed. 'Didn't realise. Expect they'll be waiting for us. Dinner will be ready.'

As they walked up the path, the lighted windows of Finmory House beckoned them in from the gathering evening. Jinny couldn't stop her feet from dancing, side-stepping, beating their own rythmn, for the circus had gone.

> '"And I was filled with such delight
> As prisoned birds must find in freedom,",' she quoted aloud.

'With such delight as Jinny Manders must find when the circus has gone.'

Then she saw Nick's pale, set face. 'Not much delight for Nick,' she thought, remembering their flat, Brandon stranded at Aunt Ag's and her parents' separation.

'I really meant it,' Jinny said. 'About coming with you next weekend to see Brandon. I'll wait 'till Dad's in a good mood, then I'll ask him to drive us over. It isn't so very far.'

'It might not be convenient,' said Nick.

'But don't you want to see him? Aren't you desperate to ride him? If it was Shantih I'd walk to Foxholm. Nothing would stop me getting to her.'

'I've told you,' said Nick. 'I just don't know if next weekend would suit.'

They reached the back door and Jinny burst into the kitchen breathing in the good smells of cooking. The long kitchen table was set. Mike, Petra and her father were already sitting round it, while Mrs Manders ladled tomato soup into bowls. Ken was standing by the sink, organising his own meal of brown rice, barley and tofu. Kelly stood watching him, his tail swinging slowly from side to side.

'Meet my family,' said Jinny to Nick, and they didn't seem like her ordinary, irritating, bossy everyday family. They were gilded people, smooth as a colour television family, bright with love for Jinny, sharing her relief that the threat of the circus had gone.

As Jinny introduced Nick, behind all the polite empty noise, the words of the poem beat their ecstatic rythmn in Jinny's head – "and I was filled with such delight'.

'One day Nick is going to jump for Britain,' she heard herself say, encouraging Nick to talk about Brandon; to tell them all that he had jumped six feet.

Any jealousy Jinny had felt towards Nick had vanished. Perhaps Nick would help her to school Shantih for show jumping; perhaps she would invite her to take Shantih with her to shows in Aunt Ag's box. And instantly Jinny was riding in a show jumping ring. She heard the starting bell and Shantih, vibrant, filled with impulsion, cantered forward. The brightly-painted, formal jumps loomed before her and fell away behind as Shantih rose on winged fetlocks to clear them effortlessly.

But Jinny only thought these things with the froth of her mind. Deep behind her heart there was the steady charm of words – "and I was filled with such delight. And I was filled with such delight".

When they had finished the meal everyone helped to wash up.

'Each plate, each knife and fork is to be thanked for the part it has played in feeding us,' said Ken. 'In cleansing them we must be aware of their service. Give them our unending gratitude.'

Often when Ken said things like that there would be an

awkward silence and someone would change the subject but tonight it seemed a perfectly normal thing to say and Jinny, drying plates saw them with a new awareness; felt the plateness of them; their patience.

Mike started to sing and they all joined in. They sang on from one song to the next and no one told Jinny she was singing out of tune or asked who had trodden on the cat. Not even Petra.

When they had finished and were all sitting round the fire Mr Manders opened a bottle of his Crab apple wine. In Jinny's glass it was the colour of fairy gold, thin, silver gold, the essence of autumn strained through translucent lime leaves. Rainbows danced on Jinny's hand through her glass.

'To Finmory,' said Mr Manders, beaming at them all from behind his red beard.

'And Shantih,' said Jinny.

'And the void,' said Ken.

Soon, Jinny thought, she would show Nick some of her paintings. But not yet, not yet.

'Shall we play Monopoly?' Mike asked hopefully, but no one answered him.

For a moment the flow of voices stopped. Jinny heard the logs on the fire sizzling, Kelly wuffing to himself in dreams.

'There's crisps in the kitchen,' said Mrs Manders and Jinny got up to go for them.

'Top shelf in the big cupboard,' her mother called after her.

Opening the cupboard, Jinny could see the packets of crisps but couldn't reach them. Grumbling to herself she went to get a stool to stand on. The stool was beside the dresser, close to the outside door. As Jinny lifted it up a letter that had been jammed between the stool and the wall fell to the floor. If there was no one about when the postman arrived he would open the back door and leave any letters on the dresser. As she bent down to pick it up, Jinny supposed that the postman had left it on the dresser that morning and somehow it had fallen down behind the stool.

Her mind still on the crisps, expecting the letter to be addressed to her father, Jinny glanced at the envelope. It was a large envelope made of expensive, pale blue paper. The handwriting of the address sprawled with bold confident letters. It read :-

Girl with long red hair,
Seen riding a chestnut Arabian mare,
On Inverburgh road,
Near GLENBOST,
Inverburgh,
Scotland

THIS LETTER IS URGENT. PLEASE DO YOUR BEST TO DELIVER IT, was written on the top left-hand corner.

On the back of the envelope was the address of the sender :-

Mrs. Muriel Raynor,
Talisker Arabian Stud,
Thane,
Dorset.

Jinny stared at the name. She was sure she didn't know a Mrs Raynor and had never heard of the Talisker Arabian Stud. She tore open the envelope and took out two sheets of matching notepaper covered with the same sprawling handwriting.

Dear Madam,

Four years ago one of my Arabian mares was stolen from my stud. Despite all investigations I have been unable to trace her. Our last clue was that a mare resembling my Wildfire had been seen in a travelling circus. This was over three years ago and I was unable to discover any more details.

Earlier this week my groom was on a coach going to Inverburgh when he saw a girl riding a chestnut Arab. He was sure she was of Talisker breeding and almost positive that she was Wildfire.

I am sending this letter in the hope that it will reach a girl with long red hair and by some miraculous chance the chestnut she was riding will turn out to be my own Wildfire.

My mare had a white mark the size of a five pence piece behind her right ear, though it is possible that this may have grown out by now.

I cannot tell you how wonderful it would be to find Wildfire after all this time.

Should this letter reach you, please contact me at the above address.

Yours sincerely,
Muriel Raynor.

Jinny stood motionless, hardly breathing, staring down at the letter she read it over and over again. Jinny knew every inch of Shantih. She was positive that she didn't have a white mark. Positive. Pushing the letter into her pocket she grabbed a torch from the dresser and raced outside.

Flinging herself over the field gate and stumbling across the grass she ran to her horse, to Shantih. Not Wildfire of Talisker but Shantih.

Her hand holding the torch trembled as she pushed back Shantih's mane from behind her right ear. For a minute Jinny could see nothing, no white mark that would have branded Shantih into Wildfire but as she looked more closely she saw that amongst the short chestnut hairs there was a dusting of white hairs. Holding the torch between shoulder and chin Jinny plucked out the offending hairs and let them fall on the grass. She worked steadily, ignoring Shantih's objections.

'There,' she said at last. 'No one would know now.'

'But you know,' answered the voice in her head. 'You know.'

CHAPTER SIX

When Jinny went back into the house she stood for a moment in the kitchen, clutching her arms about herself, bracing herself to face her family's sympathy.

'Is that you?' called her mother and Jinny went through to the sitting room.

'Where have you been?' demanded Petra.

'What's wrong?' asked her mother, knowing from Jinny's white face and shocked expression that something had happened.

'It's this. The postman must have left it on the dresser. It had fallen down behind the stool,' Jinny said, producing the letter from her pocket.

She unfolded it and began to read it aloud but her voice shook so much that her father had to take it from her and continue reading it.

'Oh Jinny!' cried her mother when Mr Manders had finished. 'What a dreadful shock for you! I can't believe it.'

'D'you mean she could take Shantih away?' cried Mike. 'Just come and claim her. That is *if* Shantih is this woman's horse.'

'Well, yes, I think she could,' said Mr Manders slowly. 'She would be within her rights. If she could prove Shantih was her horse.'

'I doubt very much if she could do that,' said Jinny's mother, trying desperately to think of something comforting to say.

'Does Shantih have the white mark?' demanded Petra. 'Have you looked? Does she have it?'

''Course I've looked and she doesn't have it,' said Jinny, for there was no white mark left on Shantih now.

'Write and tell her that,' said Mrs Manders. 'That proves Shantih isn't her horse. I'm quite sure it is all a mistake. Maybe she's some crackpot who is just trying it on.'

'She does say her horse had been seen in a circus,' said Petra. 'And Shantih did come from a circus.'

Jinny stared at her sister, thinking that it was quite unbelievable how Petra always had to say the thing that everyone else was thinking but tactfully not saying.

'That proves nothing,' said Mike. 'Not a thing. Anyway we won't let this Raynor woman near Shantih. Jinny can hide in the hills and we'll tell this Raynor Rat that Jinny has gone to boarding school and Shantih was sold to a dealer, or broke a leg and had to be shot.'

For a second Jinny clutched at her brother's words. She could easily ride Shantih into the hills and hide there but even before Petra had commented on how much it would cost to bribe the whole of Glenbost, Jinny knew it was useless. If Shantih was Mrs Raynor's stolen Arab, now she had been seen there was nothing, absolutely nothing, that could be done to stop Mrs Raynor coming to Finmory and taking Shantih away. Once the groom had seen Shantih and Jinny had read Mrs Raynor's letter it was too late to change anything.

'Try not to upset yourself too much,' said her mother. 'It's probably a storm in a teacup. Shantih hasn't got this white mark so it really looks as if she is not Mrs Raynor's horse. And you know we'd never let her take Shantih away.'

'How could you stop her if . . .' but Jinny stuck in mid sentence. She raked her nails down her arms and twisted her toes painfully in her shoes. She knew if she started crying she wouldn't be able to stop and she could feel the silent Nick watching her intently from behind her glasses. Jinny wasn't going to cry in front of Nick if she could help it.

'Let's play Monopoly,' she said, her voice unnaturally high.

Mike sprang to his feet.

'Good idea,' he said, hurrying to his bedroom to find the Monopoly.

'It will be all right, dear,' said her mother. 'This kind of thing just can't happen.'

'Oh yes it can,' said Nick staring into the fire. 'Yes it can.'

They played Monopoly until after midnight when Mrs Manders, declaring it was a draw between Mike and Ken, said it was time they were all in bed.

'Nick would have to be here tonight,' Jinny thought. All she wanted was to be alone.

'What's the painting?' Nick asked, standing in front of the mural that was painted on the wall of Jinny's room.

'The Red Horse,' said Jinny. 'A tinker woman painted it. I helped her.'

'Weird,' said Nick.

'Yes,' said Jinny, for the Red Horse was linked with Shantih, with Jinny herself and with the Tinker folk; and all were linked to an even more ancient mystery. The power of the Red Horse had saved Jinny from drowning; had led her to a Celtic statuette buried on the moors, but tonight there was no power in the Horse. It was no more than a painting of a red horse charging through green leaves, its yellow eyes flat, without life.

Jinny undressed quickly, said goodnight to Nick and got into bed, pulling the bedclothes over her head. Lying in the darkness would have been the time for talking, but, listening to Nick getting into the camp bed, Jinny said nothing, pretended to be asleep.

Once Jinny was sure that Nick was sleeping she emerged from under the bedclothes. Lying flat on her back she was so tense that she seemed to be floating inches above the mattress.

'She is going to take Shantih away from me. Come here and take Shantih away,' Jinny told herself, and it was as if the future were the past and Shantih had gone back to the Talisker stud. It had happened; it was in the past.

Jinny lay all night without sleeping. She was afraid to sleep in case when she woke up she would have forgotten what had happened and would have to bear the shock of Mrs Raynor's letter all over again.

During the night Jinny thought of all the pony book solutions – cutting off Shantih's mane and dying her black so that Mrs Raynor wouldn't recognise her; or riding her down to England to stay with a friend; or barricading the road to Finmory so that Mrs Raynor couldn't get through, but with an aching emptiness Jinny knew that she couldn't really do any of these things. Mrs Raynor would come and inspect Shantih. Jinny was certain that Shantih was Wildfire of Talisker. Mrs Raynor's groom had known her, she had been in a circus and the white hairs that Jinny had plucked out of Shantih's coat had been all that remained of the distinguishing white spot that had grown there when Shantih was younger.

Tears drained out of the corners of Jinny's eyes, running slowly down her face and soaking her pillow.

'Please don't let it happen. Please, please let me keep Shantih,' she prayed silently, asking hopelessly for what seemed impossible. 'Please God, not Shantih. She's mine.'

At last the room grew lighter. The night was nearly over. Jinny did not know how she could get up and go on listening to her family being sympathetic, or what she could find to say to Nick, when Nick had Brandon and Shantih was going to be taken away from her.

Nick stirred restlessly in the camp bed, then sat up. Through the slit of her half-closed eyes, Jinny saw her get up and cross to the window that looked out over the horses' field to the sea. She stood without moving for several minutes, staring through the window, then, still looking out to Finmory Bay, she said, 'It's all lies about Dad working in England, looking for a house for us, about Aunt Ag keeping Brandon. I made it all up.'

'You mean you don't have a pony?' gasped Jinny, jumping up, forgetting that she was pretending to be asleep. 'There's no Brandon? But the photographs in your room?'

'Brandon's at Aunt Ag's all right,' said Nick, and as she turned to Jinny her face was the same tense, tear-stained mask that Jinny had seen from the bus. 'But I've got to sell him. We've no money. Mum doesn't work for an advertising agency. Made that up too. She's only got a temporary job in a supermarket and when that's finished goodness knows when she'll get anything else.'

'Your father?'

'They're getting divorced. He hasn't any money either. His firm went bankrupt. He's nothing left. I don't really understand what happened. Don't want to know. But they took the house and just about everything else. I thought they were going to be able to take Brandon but he was mine so they couldn't touch him. Not that it would have made much difference. He's got to go now. Least Aunt Ag is trying to find him a good home. I want him to go to somewhere where he can go on show jumping. He's too good to go to a pet home.'

'You mean you'll never see him again?'

'I'll see him next weekend. I just couldn't bear to go and ride him this weekend, knowing I had to sell him. Aunt Ag put an ad. in this week's *Scottish Farmer*. Anyone who sounds suitable will be coming to see him next Saturday. I'll be there. Just a chance that one of Aunt Ag's friends might be interested in him. Then I could keep in touch. Someday buy him back. Ha! Bloomin' Ha! That will be bloomin' right!'

'I knew about your parents splitting up. Mr Lawson told me the day he was asking me to show you round,' admitted Jinny.

'You knew!' exclaimed Nick. 'Well you might have said.'

'I didn't get the chance to begin with and then I couldn't, not when you'd told me such . . .'

'I do it all the time,' interrupted Nick. 'I'm always lying. Won't matter when I'm jumping for Britain. That's what's so rotten about the whole filthy mess. Brandon's my special horse, my Olympic horse. We were going to the top together. Other riders have done it on ponies smaller than Brandon.'

'The same way as Shantih's my special horse. I was sure that when I came to Finmory I would find her here. I'd been searching for Shantih all my life. How can a complete stranger come and take her away? How can they, when I love her so much?'

'Don't know,' said Nick. 'But if she is Wildfire they will take her. Your father was quite sure that they had the right to reclaim her. The same as someone will come and take Brandon away next weekend.'

'But you could refuse to sell him. Wouldn't your Aunt

Ag keep him for you? You could pay her back, work for her in the holidays?'

'No,' said Nick. 'We've got to have the money. Got to have it to pay for that stinking flat. I don't mean we haven't much money. I mean we haven't any. And you've seen Mum how worried she is about it all. I can't stand seeing her going crazy, so that's that.'

Nick and Jinny stared at each other despairingly.

'If only I hadn't been on the Inverburgh road when that coach passed. Five minutes and I'd have been off the road. Three minutes even, and he'd never have seen us. It would have made no difference to them. Years since she was stolen from them. Years. Bet Mrs Raynor had forgotten all about her. Bet she has masses of Arabs. Just names to her.'

'If only Dad hadn't got fed up with us,' said Nick wearily. 'His business would still have gone bust but at least we would have been together. Mum would have had him. I can't bear it when she sits staring at me, all worried and miserable. Both of us sitting there trying to pretend that everything's fine and nothing's happened. I can't bear the way she keeps on saying she'll make it up to me. As if anything could make up for having to sell Brandon.' Nick turned away to stare out of the window again.

'I couldn't live without Shantih . . .' began Jinny.

Suddenly Nick sprang away from the window. She stood at the foot of Jinny's bed, running her splayed fingers through her cropped hair.

'Don't!' she yelled. 'We mustn't go on like this. I am going to jump for Britain and NOTHING will stop me. Give in now and we've had it. Let them beat us now and all the black things have won. If I can't keep Brandon I'll find another show jumper. I'm going to the top. You'll see.'

'I only want to have Shantih,' began Jinny.

'Well I don't. There's no "only's" for me. I want everything. When you jump a difficult fence and you feel the crowd holding its breath and the gasp when you're safely over, that's what I want. Riding against the clock, going faster than you dare and yet being dead accurate. Knowing every split second counts, risking it but not too much. Nothing existing in the whole world but the challenge of the jumps and the applause.'

Jinny listened entranced. Nick sparkled with energy. As she spoke Jinny could almost hear the pound of galloping hooves; could feel Shantih flying round a course of show jumps to thunder through the finish, a clear round behind her, the burst of applause making her buck – head down, heels high – in delight at her own brilliance.

'And it's the people,' went on Nick. 'They're so different to ordinary, dull, everyday people. They're chancers. They don't care about anything except how their horse is jumping. Don't care about being respectable or polite or what they look like. They live in a different world and I'm going to be part of it. Nothing is going to stop me. You'll see.'

After breakfast Mrs Manders made Jinny sit down and reply to Mrs Raynor's letter.

'Darling, you will have to write. I know it's dreadful for you but putting it off won't do any good.'

How can I write to her and tell her about Shantih? It's like writing to her and asking her to come and take Shantih away.'

'You must,' said Petra who always seemed to be ready with her rent-a-conscience service at the least excuse.

'Leave me alone,' stormed Jinny. 'It's got nothing to do with you, so leave me alone.'

'That shows you know I'm right,' said Petra, collecting her music and departing to her piano.

'I can't let anyone come and take Shantih away.'

'Reply to the letter. Then we can see. If Shantih hasn't got the white mark I should think they've got the wrong horse. The groom fellow could only have caught a glimpse of her from the coach. I should think that one chestnut horse seen from a coach would look pretty much the same as any other,' said Mr Manders.

Grimly Jinny found notepaper and a pen and settled herself to write. All chestnut horses looked much the same to her father but Jinny knew that she could have picked Shantih out from a hundred chestnut Arabs. If she had been the groom she would have recognised her horse.

When the letter was finished it read:

Dear Mrs Raynor,

I received your letter yesterday. Although I do have a chestnut Arab there is no possible chance of her being your stolen horse. She does not have any white mark behind her ear. I bought her several years ago from a farmer who is now dead. He bred her himself.

Yours sincerely,

Jennifer Manders.

Nick had helped her to write it.

'A hundred more years in hell,' Jinny thought as she sealed the envelope quickly in case her parents should want to see the letter. She didn't care how many lies she had to tell as long as it stopped Mrs Raynor coming to Finmory to inspect Shantih.

In the afternoon Nick and Jinny rode Bramble and Shantih to Mr MacKenzie's field.

'It all looks the same,' Jinny thought. 'How can anything be the same as it was yesterday before I got that letter?'

Yesterday's evening of firelight and laughter had fallen over the edge of Jinny's world as if it had never been. She felt tears stinging in her eyes as she ran her hand down Shantih's satin neck. But it was not Shantih she was riding. It was Wildfire of Talisker who belonged to Mrs Raynor. Jinny could not believe it was possible.

'Better do a bit of schooling first,' said Nick, already walking Bramble round the edge of the field. 'Let them know they're being ridden.'

Jinny nodded. Normally she would have been worried about churning up Mr MacKenzie's good ground, especially on the Sabbath when the MacKenzies thought everyone should attend church and sit at home reading their Bibles. But today she didn't care. Gathering Shantih together she eased her into a slow, sitting trot.

'Right?' asked Nick when they had been schooling for about twenty minutes. 'Shall I try and resurrect the jumps? Here, you take Bramble while I bash them together.'

In no time Nick had reorganised poles, bales and drums into four reasonable-sized jumps.

'How's that?' she asked, taking Bramble back and remounting.

Jinny was about to say that never in a year of Sundays would Bramble think of going near jumps that size, when she remembered it was Nick who was riding him and had the sense to say nothing.

Jinny watched Nick digging her heels into Bramble's hairy sides, driving him into his bit with her seat and legs. He cleared the first two jumps, using his quarters as he took off and stretching out over the jumps to land smoothly without his usual spine-shattering jolt. Nick could ride.

'He'd make a smashing cross country pony,' she said.

'With you on top,' agreed Jinny.

'Your turn.'

Jinny rode Shantih towards the jumps. For a moment she felt self-conscious, aware of Nick watching her, but feeling Shantih's trot change into her smooth canter and her ears prick forward, Jinny forgot everything except her horse and the delight of jumping.

Shantih glided golden over the jumps, taking off, soaring and landing far beyond the churn of Bramble's hoofprints. Over the last two jumps her canter became a gallop and the heaped obstacles so insignificant that, to Jinny, Shantih seemed to soar for the sheer joy of it.

'Can't she jump,' Nick exclaimed as Jinny rode back to her with a grin stretching her mouth from ear to ear. 'And doesn't she love it! What a horse!'

'Could jump the moon,' said Jinny.

'Let's build her a decent jump.' Nick sprang down from Bramble and threw her reins to Jinny.

Working furiously she changed the second two jumps into one spread of about four feet.

'Super,' said Jinny, full of confidence that Shantih would clear it.

She cantered Shantih in a circle, took her over the first two jumps again, turned, checked, and sitting down hard drove Shantih at the jump. A stride before Jinny was expecting it, Shantih took off. Jinny jack-knifed, letting the reins slip through her fingers as Shantih stretched to clear the jump and land far out on the other side.

'She could,' shouted Nick. 'Honest she could.'

'Could what?' demanded Jinny as she struggled to bring Shantih back to a trot and a calmer frame of mind.

'Could show jump,' declared Nick. 'She hardly noticed that. It was nothing to her. She's over 14·2 so you'd need to register with B.S.J.A. as a Junior Associate Member, and jump in adult classes, but I bet she'd win. Need to school like mad to settle her down, stop her going bananas every time she sees a jump but I bet you she'd make it.'

The dream of a red rosette, of coloured poles, of thunderous applause, shone brilliant in Jinny's imagination. Not a few jumps at a cattle show but proper show jumping against top show jumpers; the harsh electric light of an indoor arena glinting on snaffle ring and stirrup iron; the sharp gasp of breath from the crowd as she rode Shantih at a looming red wall.

The sound of voices and footsteps splashing along the muddy track on the other side of the hedge, jolted Jinny back to mundane reality. At first she thought it must be Mr MacKenzie coming to complain about the damage they were doing to his ground, then she recognised her father's voice but not the woman's voice that answered him.

Mr Manders reached the field gate, pushed it open and stood back to let a middle-aged woman wearing green wellies, green cords, a green anorak and an expensive green headscarf tied round her long horsy face and grey hair, walk through the gate in front of him. Three Jack Russell terriers bounced at her heels.

'This is Jinny,' said her father. 'And this is the horse you are interested in.'

Sky and field swam fluid about Jinny. She clutched at Shantih's mane, pressed her head down to her knees and felt Nick grab her shoulder.

'S'O.K.,' she said and with her arms round Shantih's neck she slid to the ground and stood leaning against Shantih until the landscape settled again. She could not imagine how Mrs Raynor had tracked her down so quickly. If she could prove that Shantih was Wildfire did it mean she could take her away now?

'Jinny,' introduced her father. 'This is Miss Trevor, a friend of Mrs Raynor's. She has driven over to see Shantih.'

Miss Trevor thrust a wrinkled, bony hand at Jinny and said, 'How de do,' more through her pinched nostrils than through the lipless slit of her mouth. 'Muriel Raynor phoned me up and told me the news about her groom spotting Wildfire. When I heard where he'd seen her I promised I'd do a little detective work, see if I could track her down and here I am. Not many Arabs in Glenbost. So this is Muriel's mare?'

'This is Shantih,' stated Jinny.

'Quite,' said Miss Trevor. 'I am totally sympathetic. Do realise that this whole business must have come as a terrible shock to you but Muriel was so fond of Wildfire. She has never stopped searching, so I do feel that if this is her horse we must let her know. Now, what did she tell me? White spot behind her right ear. Can I look?'

Before Jinny realised what was happening Miss Trevor had lifted the headpiece of Shantih's bridle at her right ear and her long, twitching fingers were searching for any white mark.

'Nothing there,' she announced and Jinny's heart thumped with relief.

'Of course not,' said Jinny. 'If you'd waited a minute I was just going to tell you that she doesn't have a white spot. She is not Mrs Raynor's . . .'

'But what's this?' cried Miss Trevor, interrupting Jinny, her excitement setting off her terriers into demented yapping. 'Look! Not a spot but quite a few white hairs. Now this is hopeful. Muriel will be so delighted.'

'There aren't any,' cried Jinny but her voice dried in her throat, for where Miss Trevor had parted the hair close to Shantih's mane there was a sprinkling of white hairs that

Jinny must have missed last night. Not expecting anyone to come to inspect Shantih so soon, Jinny had not bothered to check again.

'All her other markings are identical to Wildfire's,' said Miss Trevor, 'so this does look promising. Not too well up in Arab's myself, but Muriel will know the second she sees her. She'll be eternally grateful to find her in such super condition.'

'Nothing to be grateful about,' said Jinny. 'Shantih is mine.'

'Lord,' exclaimed Miss Trevor. 'It is all going to be very difficult. Naturally Mrs Raynor will want to see her for herself.'

'Shantih is jumping at Ardair Show at the end of November,' stated Nick. 'Even if she is her horse Mrs Raynor couldn't possibly take her away before that.'

Jinny's mouth fell open at Nick's jumbo lie. Ardair was an indoor show held under BSJA rules. In her wildest ambitions Jinny had never thought of taking Shantih to it.

'Jumping at Ardair? Jolly good!' exclaimed Miss Trevor, obviously as amazed as Jinny. 'Haven't seen her jumping at any shows before.'

'She wasn't ready before,' said Nick.

'But I've seen you, haven't I? Gathering in the pots on that little bay of yours?'

'Brandon,' said Nick.

'The one. Well, I'll be on the phone to Muriel tonight. Give her all the gen. Up to her what she does next but if you're entered for Ardair . . . Pretty sporting effort. Muriel will appreciate that and she will be so pleased to know that her horse has been so well looked after.'

'MY horse,' declared Jinny. 'Shantih is mine. Not Mrs Raynor's.'

But Miss Trevor had already started to splodge her way out of the field.

That evening Jinny rewrote her letter to Mrs Raynor, leaving out the last sentence. There was no point in lying. Her father had told Miss Trevor how Shantih had come from a circus. Miss Trevor would have told Mrs Raynor.

'Shantih jump at Ardair!' Jinny thought as she walked slowly down to say Good night to Shantih and Bramble. Ardair show was held in a big, indoor arena about forty miles from Inverburgh. Ever since Claire Burnley had told her about it, Jinny had always longed to go to it; had never thought of jumping in it. Nick was mad if she thought Shantih could ever be good enough for Ardair.

For a second the dream of show jumping flared brilliant in Jinny's mind; for a second she was astride Shantih, riding her into the arena at Ardair. High-stepping, proud, Shantih danced into the barricade of spotlights, the tan flirting from beneath her eager hooves. In Jinny's ears there was the reverberation of the commentator's voice announcing, 'Miss Jennifer Manders riding her own horse, Shantih.'

And instantly the dream had vanished, for Shantih was not her own horse, did not belong to Jinny.

CHAPTER SEVEN

It was Thursday morning before Nick said any more about Brandon having to be sold. Although she still talked endlessly about her pony, she had said nothing more about the necessity of selling him and not another word about her parents' divorce, so that Jinny was almost beginning to wonder if she had dreamed their conversation.

When she had asked Nick how her mother was, Nick had only said, 'Fine,' and changed the subject quickly and obviously.

'Be that way,' Jinny had thought, and gone back to worrying about Shantih. There had been no further word from Mrs Raynor and, as all Jinny's family kept telling her, there was nothing more to be done until they heard from her again. Nothing that was, except spend every free minute with Shantih; nothing except telling herself over and over again that no one could ever take Shantih away from her; nothing except trying to break the future with Ken's positive thinking, when all the time the future was blank and empty, unthinkable without Shantih.

'You are coming tomorrow, aren't you?' Nick said after school on Thursday afternoon. They were both in the cloakroom and Jinny was struggling to pull on her jodhs under her skirt.

'What? To your Aunt Ag's?' asked Jinny, wriggling out of her skirt and pushing her feet back into her shoes. 'But you never asked me. Not properly.'

'I did. Aunt Ag is picking us up here tomorrow. You said you'd come.'

'But . . .' began Jinny, not looking at Nick. She wanted to say that she couldn't come, couldn't leave Shantih for a whole weekend. Yet it wasn't just an ordinary invitation, it was Nick asking Jinny to be with her while she sold her horse.

'Come,' said Nick.

'Is it yourself that is ready?' Dolina demanded, picking up Jinny's school bag. 'It is the mystery to me what you would be at without me to hold you together.'

'Oh O.K., then,' Jinny said to Nick. 'Though I should stay with Shantih.' Tugging on her cagoule she raced after Dolina.

There was no letter from Mrs Raynor waiting for Jinny at Finmory.

'Perhaps she's had a heart attack,' Jinny said, making her mother tut her tongue as Jinny had known she would.

'I don't want to go to Nick's Aunt Ag,' Jinny told her family. 'The very last thing I want to do is spend the weekend watching Nick selling Brandon but I suppose I'll have to.'

'She's often late,' Nick said as they waited for Aunt Ag on Friday afternoon.

The playground was deserted, the staff car park almost empty, the only light left on in the school was in the janitor's room.

'Something must have happened.'

It was another half hour before Aunt Ag arrived. She was driving a large, battered, horse box.

'Sorry, girls,' she said as they climbed into the cabin. 'Picked up a youngster from Bob Morgan's. The crazy coot got out of his halter. Played ring-a-roses with me all round the box before I could get him tied up again.'

Aunt Ag was large and blonde. Her blue eyes twinkled from webs of laughter lines. Her nose was snub, her cheeks rosy, her full lips smiled back from protruding tombstone teeth. Her fuzzy hair was held in a bun at the nape of her neck. She wore an ancient Barbour jacket, stained and torn. On her feet she had a pair of men's wellingtons.

'You're Jinny,' she said, squashing Jinny's hand in a powerful paw. 'Glad to meet you. Decent of you to come over with Nick. Help us all to keep a stiff upper lip while we walk through hell?'

The lane leading up to Aunt Ag's house was lined with tall trees, bright in the beams of the headlights against the dark sky, and when they drove in to the stable yard the lights from a range of loose boxes shone golden, silhouetting arched necks and eager heads, whinnying in answer to the youngster's frantic, blurting neighs coming from the confines of the horse box.

A boy of about seventeen, dark as Aunt Ag was fair, came running across the yard, closely followed by an eight-year-old double of Aunt Ag. From Nick's many stories about her cousins Jinny recognized them as Richard and Steph.

'Did you get him?' the boy asked.

'The begger broke loose. Some carry-on I had trying to persuade him to put his head back in the halter. Wish you luck with this one.'

'Richard schools difficult horses,' explained Nick as they jumped down in to the yard.

Steph launched herself at Nick, throwing her arms round her neck, and nearly knocking her glasses off.

'I've been looking after Brandon,' she said. 'I've talked

to him every day and taken him sugar and apples and explained to him over and over again about it not being your fault and how you're going to find a good home for him until you can buy him back.'

Aunt Ag and Richard were already lowering the ramp to the accompaniment of clattering hooves and shrill whinnyings.

Jinny stood back, feeling suddenly left out. She looked round at the stable yard and buildings. Everything was spotless – fresh paint on the boxes and not so much as a wisp of straw in the yard. She walked across to one of the boxes and spoke to a clipped grey mare who stood on a thick straw bed with a full haynet hanging at the back of her box. Jinny went down the row of six loose boxes and all the horses were as well set up as the grey.

'It doesn't make sense,' Jinny thought. If Aunt Ag could afford to keep her horses like this why couldn't she lend money to Mrs Webster and let Nick keep Brandon? Having another pony at grass would hardly be noticed here.

The youngster clattered down the ramp, pirouetted around Richard and stood up on his hind legs. He was a scrawny black, showing too much white in his left eye. His mane and tail was straggly, as if he had been sharing a field with calves.

'I'll keep him in for tonight,' Richard said and led him away.

'Want to see Brandon?' Nick offered, her voice casual.

'Desperate,' said Jinny, and followed Nick and Steph past a feed house and tack room to older stabling out of sight of the main yard.

Brandon, looking exactly like his photographs, was standing pulling at a haynet.

'Fatso,' said Nick. 'Gutzying as usual.'

At the sound of Nick's voice the bay pony skittered to the box door, sharp whinnyings bursting from his nostrils. He pushed against the door and when Nick went into the box he rubbed against her, smelling at her pocket, breathing over her face and leaning his head on her shoulder.

'Get off,' said Nick. 'What's all the fuss for?'

Her voice trembled as she spoke and she stood with her back to Jinny and Steph, dragging the sleeve of her jacket across her eyes in a swift, surreptitious movement.

He's smashing,' said Jinny going into the box beside Nick, running her hand down the short, muscled neck and hard bulk of Brandon's shoulder. Brandon searched her hands for food, and the thick lips, short, chunky head, felt all wrong after Shantih's fine bone and gentle sweetness.

'Supper in half an hour,' Aunt Ag shouted. 'Steph, give Richard a hand.'

'Sorry,' said Nick. 'Didn't introduce you. Steph this is Jinny. Jinny, Steph.'

Richard came past carrying full water buckets.

'Richard,' Nick called. 'This is Jinny.'

'Hi,' Richard called, his smile a sudden brightness in his dark face, and Jinny thought he looked more like a pop star than a horsey person.

'Want a hand!' Nick offered and they all went to fill up water buckets and feed the horses.

The first six boxes Jinny had seen, and the main yard, were obviously the show piece of the stable. The other boxes and range of stalls were less affluent. Their wooden doors were patched where past occupants had kicked them down, the stalls badly needed painting and the horses were bedded on shavings not straw. Although the horses and ponies in them were fit and well-groomed, they had not the quality of the aristocrats in the front boxes. Jinny decided that those must be show hunters or horses at full livery.

'That's everything,' said Richard, putting off the light in the feed house. 'In for supper or mother will be rampant. Hear you've got an Arab?' he said to Jinny, walking beside her.

'Shantih,' said Jinny and instantly the pit opened at her feet for she did not have an Arab called Shantih. She had only been looking after an Arab called Wildfire of Talisker, an Arab who belonged to Mrs Raynor.

Richard pushed open the door of a large utility room and a jubilation of Bearded Collies erupted at them. Blues and fawns, brown, blacks and greys bounded about them. Shaggy paws were planted on their shoulders, frantic tongues licked Jinny's face, saffron eyes gleamed with love and devotion from under falls of frosted hair, dark eyes shone under shaggy eyebrows and the row of their delight was high as a disco's mind-bending blare.

'Shut up!' Richard roared. 'Quiet! Quiet! Shut up!'

'They're all right after a minute or two,' gasped Nick, fighting off Beardies. 'They are just so friendly!'

'Gorgeous,' shouted Jinny and her mouth was filled with a suffocating mass of Beardie hair.

'Kezzy, Mall, Pandora, Rags, Tosh and Misty,' said Steph.

But to Jinny they were one vast, many-headed, multi-pawed airborne hysteric.

Holding back the dogs Richard let them in to the kitchen, where one black and white Beardie came to meet them – tail wagging, dark eyes glinting in the firelight, yapping, mumbling, smiling a welcome in the nearest thing Jinny had ever heard to Dog English.

'Meg,' said Steph. 'She's the best.'

Down on her knees stroking Meg, Jinny looked round the shadowy, stone-floored kitchen. Despite the warmth from the ancient Aga, the bowls of steaming soup waiting for them on the table, and Aunt Ag's welcome as she cut slices from a home-baked loaf – Jinny could see that the room was shabby and neglected. Curtains and matting were worn into shreds and patches; the stone sinks were chipped, the dresser, table and chairs were clawed and gnawed by generations of Beardies. Two sunken armchairs on either side of the Aga were woven over with a covering of Beardie hairs. Above the Aga a crack in the wall stretched from the cooker up to the ceiling. It was a crumbling, plaster-lipped opening – a lane to the land of the dead. Hooks behind the doors were hung with old tack. Horse blankets and a mud-clotted New Zealand rug hung from a pulley, and leg and tail bandages festooned the Aga. The room was warm and comfortable and lived-in but it wasn't the sort of kitchen that could afford to lend money to its relations.

Nick took Jinny up to their room and outside the kitchen the ice age pounced.

'Glory it is cold,' said Jinny, clutching her arms around herself and tripping on the shredded stair carpet.

'Cost a fortune to heat it,' explained Nick. 'Only the kitchen is warm but they wouldn't dream of leaving here because of the stabling and the grazing. Even Uncle Christy, who's always grumbling, wouldn't really want to live anywhere else.'

The room where Jinny and Nick were to sleep had a fungus of damp over one wall and stone hot water jars in the twin beds.

'Don't worry,' said Nick. 'Everyone takes a Beardie to bed with them.'

The bathroom made even Finmory's bathroom look modern. A rusting bath stood in regal isolation in the middle of a huge room while an ancient loo and wash basin cowered in the corners. When Jinny pulled the chain, water roared and gurgled from subterranean depths and came snorting through miles of piping to refill the cistern.

Jinny's dream that Aunt Ag could afford to lend money to her sister-in-law had vanished. It was obvious that the Websters needed all the money they had for themselves.

At the apple dumpling stage of supper Uncle Christy came in, complaining loudly about the exhaust on his car. He was a small, neat man with rimless glasses and a toothbrush moustache. He was pleasant to Jinny as he must have been to hundreds of pony-mad girls who had suddenly appeared at his table, then he retired behind his library book, spooning vaguely at his plate of soup.

'I'm going down to the stable,' Nick said when they'd all finished supper.

Jinny got up to follow her but Nick said, 'Alone,' and went out by herself.

'Gone down to see Brandon,' said Steph. 'It is the most rotten thing that could happen to anyone. Not just having to sell your own horse but having to sell Brandon when he is Nick's especial show jumper. Bet she'd have been jumping at the Horse of the Year Show next year. Bet she would. And now! We wanted to keep him here but Aunt Beryl hasn't any money. If it was my daughter I'd do anything to stop Nick having to sell Brandon. Nick even cut off her hair – I helped her do it – but she couldn't find anyone who would buy it. It's sick. It's all sick and rotten.'

'And the worst of it is I haven't been able to interest any of my friends in Brandon,' Aunt Ag said. 'If only we'd been able to trim an inch off his heels they'd have been falling over themselves to buy a brilliant 14·2 jumper for their kids. But 14·3! Takes a rider like Nick to show jump a 14·3 in adult classes.'

'Buy him for me. Please,' pleaded Steph. 'Won't be all that long until I could ride him.'

'Darling, it will be years. How about Jinny? Nick was telling us about your horse. Some total stranger trying to claim her. Brandon would be the horse for you if Shantih had to go?'

Jinny stared at Aunt Ag in blank amazement. The thought of getting another horse had never touched Jinny. There was only one horse for her – Shantih.

By ten o'clock Nick still hadn't reappeared. Aunt Ag refilled Jinny's stone hot water jar and told Meg to go to bed with her.

'You'll be fine with Meg,' Aunt Ag told her. 'And don't worry about Nick. I'll go out and see her. Expect she'll want to stay with Brandon.'

Lying in bed, the stone jar bruising her ankle bones, Meg tucked comfortingly at her back, Jinny breathed the dank air of the bedroom. She thought of the fuss there would have been at home if she had wanted to spend the night in Shantih's box. Even if, like Nick, she was being forced to sell Shantih, they would have still made a fuss.

Jinny shuddered violently, goose-over-her-grave, for it was not "if" it was "when" – *when* Mrs Raynor came for Shantih.

In the morning Nick's bed had not been slept in. When Jinny went downstairs she was sitting at the table eating a plate of porridge.

'Morning,' Nick said, grinning at Jinny, her eyes red-rimmed from sleeplessness or tears. 'First lot of buyers coming at eleven. Give us time to excercise first.'

Aunt Ag on a superb, black, show hunter led the way. Richard followed her riding a chestnut and leading the black horse that had arrived with them last night. He sat easily in the saddle, controlling the black horse with casual skill. Jinny on a clipped, sixteen-hand grey rode beside Nick who was on a dancing, high-headed, bay thoroughbred. Behind them Steph trotted along on Sparkle her show jumping pony.

A farm tractor crashed past and the black horse Richard was leading stood up on its hind legs, almost dragging its reins out of Richard's hand.

'Asking for a gallop,' Richard said, turning round to smile at Jinny once the tractor was safely past.

'Shantih is as bad,' said Jinny, feeling her spine tingling and her knees suddenly weak. Richard was really something.

'Don't,' warned Nick, knowing what Jinny was thinking. 'He has dozens of girlfriends. Everyone falls for him. It's his fatal charm.'

'Trot on,' called Aunt Ag, and as she tried to control the grey's plunging strength Jinny was brought back to earth.

The morning was bright, balanced crisply on the edge of frost, heralding winter. The trotting hooves on the road were a battalion of horse, and as they headed back towards the stables Jinny was torn between the thrill of being part of such a cavalcade, and the thought of the rest of the weekend. The thought of Brandon being loaded into a strange trailer and driven away. Behind the thought of Brandon was the unbearable thought of Shantih being driven away from Finmory in Mrs Raynor's box; of how it would be when she had to stand there and watch her being loaded.

'Punctual,' said Nick as a red Mini Traveller was driven

into the yard and two middle-aged ladies got out. One was very correctly dressed in a hacking jacket and jodhpurs; the other in a sensible tweed coat and flat-heeled shoes.

'Good morning,' said Nick as she walked across the yard. Her face was set in a smile. She was open, polite and welcoming, as if she were only going to help sell one of Aunt Ag's horses.

'Good morning,' said the tweed coat. 'I'm Miss Price and this is my sister Doris. We've arranged to see the horse you have for sale.'

'He's my horse – Brandon. Do you want him for yourselves?'

'For Doris. We've already got Grigor, our Highland, but now that Doris is really into riding, as they say, we're looking for something just a little bit better than Grigor. Not that we would dream of letting him hear us saying that.' The two women giggled like girls, beaming at Nick and Jinny, seeking their approval.

'Brandon has done a lot of show jumping,' said Nick.

'That is one of the things that attracted us to your ad. Doris has joined a Riding Club and she's planning to start jumping soon. So we want a horse who knows what it's all about, don't we Doris. Don't want two ninnies, do we?'

Looking down at her highly-polished jodhpur boots, twisting her hard hat in her hands, Doris agreed.

Aunt Ag joined them and they all went across to Brandon's box. Aunt Ag's horse dealer's patter sounded concerned and genuine but beneath its cover story Jinny could pick out the loaded darts aimed at Doris's lack of confidence – 'totally traffic proof', 'couldn't buy a more suitable Riding Club horse', 'so well-schooled and steady', 'ideal to introduce you to jumping', 'never refused in his life'.

Nick led Brandon into the yard. He stood squarely, tight and hard as a conker, watching the strangers suspiciously.

'Would you like to ride him first?' Doris mumbled.

In Aunt Ag's jumping paddock Nick sprang lightly into the saddle. She walked and trotted Brandon in circles, then cantered him around the jumps. He stayed balanced and obedient, showing no excitement at the prospect of jumping.

'Oh, doesn't she ride well,' said Doris longingly. 'I'll never be able to ride like that. Of course the whole trouble is I should have started years ago.'

'Nonsense,' declared Aunt Ag. 'It's the horse that makes all the difference. Anyone could do well on a horse like Brandon.'

Nick took Brandon over four of the smaller jumps. He cleared the jumps with efficient, workmanlike leaps, while Nick sat apparently doing nothing. In three strides after landing from the last jump, Brandon was walking calmly across to them.

Doris was reluctant to actually sit on Brandon, but was eventually persuaded by her sister to mount and ride round at a walk and trot. Her toes stuck out, her knees gaped from the saddle but her hands were light on the reins, sympathetic to Brandon's mouth.

'Sure you don't want to jump?' Aunt Ag insisted. 'He'll pop over them with you,' but Doris dropped hurriedly to the ground.

'Oh, I know he would,' she gasped. 'But I haven't started jumping yet and I might do something awful to upset him.'

'Nonsense,' brisked Aunt Ag. 'He's the very one to give you the confidence you're needing.'

'He's a lovely ride,' Doris murmured stroking Brandon's neck. 'And so well schooled. After Grigor he's bliss. Grigor just pulls all the time.'

'Well that's him. Open to any vetting you care to arrange. One hundred percent genuine. He wouldn't be for sale if circumstances had been different.'

There was a pause while Doris rummaged for more tit bits and Nick's silence lay cold and roaring about them.

'Well, I can see that Doris has fallen for him,' said the tweed coat, smiling confidentially at Aunt Ag. 'I think all we need to do now is to discuss the finance.'

'You could not make a better choice,' encouraged Aunt Ag.

'Now,' said the tweed coat, 'have you decided how much are you asking? You weren't sure when we phoned.'

'A thousand,' said Nick.

Jinny gasped aloud. If Brandon was worth a thousand pounds, a pure-bred Arab like Shantih, capable of breeding valuable foals, must be worth much more. With so much money involved there could be no hope of Mrs Raynor allowing Jinny to keep her. Jinny imagined Mrs Raynor driving to Finmory, identifying Shantih and driving her away before Jinny got home. Her last hope, that somehow her father would manage to buy Shantih, faded from Jinny's mind. Never, never, could her family afford that kind of money.

'That's rather more . . .' began the tweed coat.

'He is a show jumper,' stated Nick. 'Will be top class in a year or two.'

'I just love him,' said Doris. 'I just know I'll be able to jump if I have him.'

'There are three more parties interested in him,' said Aunt Ag. 'All coming to see him today, so discuss it and phone us after five. We shan't come to any decision before then.'

The two sisters went to have another look at Brandon

and Jinny went to phone Finmory, just in case, but there was no word from Mrs Raynor.

When Jinny went back out to the yard, the red Mini had gone. A blue Rover hatchback had taken its place. A man and a fat girl were talking to Aunt Ag while Nick was leading Brandon into the yard again.

The fat girl, who looked about eighteen, heaved herself into the saddle. Sitting sloppily, she rode Brandon round the paddock. She cantered him at a jump and was almost shot out of the saddle as Brandon cleared it. She came off at the second jump and lay mounded on the grass until Nick caught Brandon and brought him back to her. This time she stayed on for four jumps before she came off.

'That is it,' she said as she heaved herself to her feet. 'No more. I do not want a horse. I do not want to ride. If you must buy me something, buy me a moped.' She stomped back to the car.

'Two down,' said Aunt Ag as the Rover was driven away. 'What do you think?'

'Two to go,' said Nick.

The third prospective buyer was a sharp-faced woman in jeans, anorak and battered hard hat. She liked Brandon, rode and jumped him competently and said she wanted him for hunting.

'Give you a thousand for him. No messing about. Take it or leave it.' She took a cheque book from her handbag in the car.

'There's one more to see him,' said Nick.

'Bird in the hand,' mouthed Aunt Ag.

'Phone after five,' went on Nick, ignoring her Aunt.

'Was that wise?' suggested Aunt Ag as the woman drove away.

'Did you see the spurs and the cutting whip in the back of her car?' said Nick, her hand on Brandon's neck.

Mr Young arrived early. He was an elderly man, lantern-jawed, tall, scrawny. His legs, in old-fashioned breeches and black leather boots, were sparrow legs. Once, he had shown hacks, but now he showed lightweight hunters, riding with long reins, his hands tucked into his stomach. He had a small stable about thirty miles from Aunt Ag's and kept a few livery horses. Aunt Ag knew him slightly from the shows.

'Looking for a nag for the boy.' he announced in a chirruping speech. 'He's at a show today or he would have been with me.' His ball-bearing eyes darted round the yard, taking in details of wooden water buckets, clean water in the stone trough, shining tack seen through the open door of the tack room and the condition of the horses.

'He's fifteen now, high time he grew out of ponies. Want a horse to take him into Junior Associate competitions. I'm not looking for your average Pony Club hop-along. I want something that will take him to the top. Make his name for him. It's a winner I'm here to buy and nothing else. Seen you at the shows.'

'Brandon's ready to go on to the big shows now,' said Nick. 'I took him about a bit last summer and he was first in nearly every class I jumped him in.'

'Let's see him, let's see him,' demanded Mr Young.

Nick brought Brandon round into the yard and Mr Young watched, elbows wide, hands on his bent knees, as she trotted him up and down.

'Again, again. Mmm hum. Yes. Stand him up now. Stand him up.' Mr Young checked Brandon over, whispering, chirruping to him as he lifted a foreleg, pulled down an eyelid, compared the straightness of his hocks, ran experienced hands down his legs and along his back.

'Still, still, not a show horse, but that's not what I'm here for. Let's get a saddle on him.'

Aunt Ag, Richard, Jinny and Mr Young watched as Nick rode Brandon round the paddock.

'It's for the last time,' thought Jinny. 'The last real jump she'll have on him.'

But if Nick was thinking the same thing it didn't show. Her face was bright and alive. Before she had only taken Brandon over the smaller jumps, but now, for Mr Young, she rode a course over the highest show jumps. Brandon leapt, sharp-eared, bright-eyed, bouncy as a rubber ball; yet completely calm and relaxed. Jinny could not see Nick giving any aids but Brandon twisted and turned as if he could read Nick's mind.

'Hm! Hm! Hm!' Mr Young breathed his appreciation through sharp nostrils as Nick rode back to them, and asked Nick for details of Brandon's winnings.

'And who trained him for you?'

'Did it all herself,' said Aunt Ag. 'Touch of encouragement from me. But that was all.'

'Crying disgrace she has to sell him,' said Richard and walked away.

'I'll take him,' trilled Mr Young. 'He's what I want.'

'We've to talk it over,' said Nick. 'I've had other offers for him.'

'Phone me, then,' agreed Mr Young, handing Nick his card. 'Tell me your best offer and I'll top it.'

When Mr Young had gone, Aunt Ag made tea and cut a home-baked fruit cake. They sat around the kitchen table fending off drooling Beardies.

'Shouldn't be surprised if he offered fifteen hundred,' said Richard.

Jinny didn't know what she would do if she were Nick. 'I

wouldn't let Shantih go to him,' she decided. 'Not for two thousand pounds. He only wants a show jumping machine, wants the boy he talked about to win cups and rosettes. He doesn't care, not about Brandon.'

Nick finished her tea. Turned the mask of her face to Aunt Ag. 'Mr Young,' she stated.

'Doris would love him,' Jinny cried. 'He'd have a good home with them. They'd never sell him.'

'They'd be knitting bedsocks for him,' snapped Nick. 'He'd never jump again if he went to them.'

'Who is the boy Mr Young wants Brandon for?' asked Richard. 'Don't you know him from the shows?'

Nick shook her head. 'Don't know anyone called Young.'

'You've decided, then?' asked Aunt Ag. 'Reg Young knows what he's doing with a horse. Brandon will do all right with him.'

'Yes,' said Nick. 'That's it,' and she lifted up her half-empty teacup, 'To Brandon's show jumping future,' she said.

In the evening Aunt Ag phoned Mr Young. The sisters had already phoned to offer nine hundred pounds. Aunt Ag told Mr Young they had offered twelve hundred and he offered thirteen hundred. Aunt Ag accepted.

'I'll bring the cheque with me tomorrow morning when I come to collect him,' he promised.

'He's here,' Steph yelled the next morning, dashing into the kitchen where Nick and Jinny were dragging out the last of the washing up, filling in the dead time.

'Good,' said Nick. 'Get it over with,' and she smiled as Mr Young and Aunt Ag followed Steph into the kitchen.

Aunt Ag took Mr Young's cheque and Nick went back into the yard with them.

'To help them load Brandon,' Jinny thought. 'And that's it. She's sold her horse. Not hers any longer. Belongs to Mr Young.' Jinny stood in the middle of the kitchen clutching a tea towel and a half-dried plate. 'I couldn't,' she thought. 'I can't.'

Abandoning plate and towel she raced outside. She could see no one and made her way to Brandon's box. Nick was standing with her arms round Brandon, her face drained, her dark eyes blazing.

'Did you see him?' she cried to Jinny. 'The boy who is to jump Brandon? It's Liam Orme. He's Mr Young's grandson. I never knew. I never thought. Not when their names are different.'

'What's wrong with him?'

'You've only to look at him. He rides as if he's steering a double decker bus. Sits there like a ton of potatoes.' Nick stared in blank dismay at Jinny.

'Tell them you've changed your mind.'

'He's paid Aunt Ag the cheque and we need the money. Mum's got to have the money this week.'

'But if he's going to be cruel to Brandon?'

'He won't be cruel, not R.S.P.C.A. cruel. He'll batter him round the shows until he's knocked the stuffing out of him and sell him on.'

'Then don't sell him. Tear up the cheque,' cried Jinny.

'They're ready to load him,' said Richard, coming to the box door. 'Want me to take him?'

'I'll do it,' said Nick, blowing her nose hard.

She put a rope halter on Brandon who walked wide-eyed, startled by the storm of emotion, skittering on his oiled hooves, his blocky head high.

In the yard Nick gave Brandon's rope to Mr Young who began to lead him into the float. Liam came up behind them, swinging his arms, shouting, waving a stick and Brandon sprang into the trailer.

'Bit of life there,' Liam said, grinning at Nick. His fleshy face was lurid with acne and his wet lips showed decayed teeth.

He looked about fifteen years old. Not tall but big, bursting out of his jeans and scarlet body warmer. The sleeves of his navy sweater were pushed up over his elbows, his hands with their grimy, bitten nails broke the stick into pieces as he spoke.

Nick turned her back on him.

'Sorry, but that's life. Can't hold one hand out for the cash and hold on to your darling pony with the other.'

'Leave her alone,' swore Jinny. 'You've got her horse, so shut up.'

'Oh, temper, temper,' Liam mocked. 'Who has the red hair, then? Don't know what all her fuss is about. She'll still be seeing him. No more pussy footing about, now he's got me to ride him. We'll be for the big time. You'll both be coming to see us at Ardair? Give us a little cheer when we win?'

Nick, Richard, Aunt Ag and Jinny stood watching as the float was driven away.

'Oh well,' said Richard awkwardly, but Aunt Ag pulled Nick to her in a giant bear-hug, comforting her without words.

'Perhaps you will be able to buy him back. Perhaps things will change,' said Jinny without hope.

'How about jumping Moses for me in the 14·2 jumping at Gavinton a week on Saturday?' Aunt Ag asked. 'You can look on him as yours. Gather in a few more pots before adulthood overtakes you?'

Nick shook her head decisively. 'No,' she said. 'But I'll

come to Gavinton. Jinny is going to jump Shantih and I'm their trainer.'

'Good idea,' agreed Aunt Ag. 'Why not?'

'Because . . .' began Jinny, so many reasons why she was not going to show jump Shantih jostling in her mind that she could hardly find words for any of them. 'Because Mrs Raynor will be coming to see her.'

'And you are just going to pine away, waiting for her to arrive?' demanded Nick. 'You heard what that Miss Trevor said, "Jolly sporting of you to be jumping Shantih at Ardair." Dare say Mrs Raynor will be so impressed if you win at Ardair she'll let you keep Shantih.'

'Win at Ardair,' gasped Jinny. 'Don't be crazy. We're not nearly good enough to compete at Ardair, never mind think about winning.'

'You will be, with me to train you,' promised Nick, and it might have been years since she sold Brandon. She was charged with new energy, full face forward, towards the new challenge of turning Jinny and Shantih into show jumpers.

Jinny felt a total admiration for Nick. Nick hid her heartbreak beneath a mask of indifference. Brandon had been sold and that was that. For a second Jinny wondered if it was only winning that mattered to Nick; if she didn't care about Brandon. Yet Jinny had seen Nick crying over Brandon's photograph and knew that this wasn't true.

'You'll win a red rosette at Ardair,' promised Nick.

For a moment the video inside Jinny's head switched from Mrs Raynor instantly recognising Shantih and producing irrefutable evidence to prove that she was Wildfire of Talisker to the surge of applause that followed her round the ring at Ardair, a red rosette fluttering proudly from Shantih's bridle.

And Jinny wondered suddenly if this might be a way through. If she set her heart on winning at Ardair Show it might cover up the agony of losing Shantih. It might help her to wear the mask so close to her skin that no one would know what she was really feeling.

'Anyway,' said Nick. 'You will jump her at Gavinton. It's only a potty little Club show but it will do to start with.'

'Anyway,' echoed Jinny grimly. 'We'll need to wait until I hear from Mrs Raynor. She may want to take Shantih back at once.'

CHAPTER EIGHT

The reply from Mrs Raynor reached Finmory by Tuesday's post. It was waiting for Jinny when she got home from detention. She stood staring at the envelope with the bold handwriting. Reading it with X-ray eyes she was sure that it said, 'I shall be in Scotland next week and shall come to Finmory to reclaim my horse.'

Jinny turned away without even touching it. She took off her boots, cagoule and scarf and put them away tidily.

'It's arrived,' said her mother, coming into the kitchen.

'I see it,' said Jinny. Swinging her school bag on her shoulder, she picked up the letter between finger and thumb and set off to her room.

'Well?' called her father, seeing Jinny going upstairs.

Jinny didn't reply but went steadily on. In her room she dumped her school bag on the floor. Holding the letter bomb, flat and explosive between the palms of her hands, she stared out through the heavy grey light down to the horses's field. She could just make out Bramble's bulked shape but it was only when Shantih moved that Jinny could see her. It was as if Mrs Raynor was weaving spells from the height of her dark Talisker tower and drawing Shantih towards her.

'When I read her letter,' Jinny thought, 'she will have power here at Finmory. Shantih will belong more to her than to me.'

She took the letter and went to stand in front of the Red Horse. There was a tightness in her throat and her hands trembled as she tore open the envelope and unfolded the sheets of deckle-edged note paper. A photograph fluttered, face downwards, to the floor but Jinny ignored it. She stared at the flamboyant handwriting but it was seconds before the indented scrawls and loops shaped themselves into words and she was able to read it.

Dear Miss Manders,

I cannot tell you how truly delighted I was to receive your letter, and to hear from my friend, Miss Trevor, that your Arab came from a circus and bears a striking resemblance to my own stock. We have been searching for her for years. Never giving up hope. I enclose a photograph taken when Wildfire was three years old, six months before she was stolen.

I cannot wait to see her for myself, but am under doctor's orders to take things easy for a while. I fly out to Florida tomorrow to spend two months in the sun. Miss Trevor tells me that you are jumping Wildfire at Ardair Show. I had already arranged to stay with Miss Trevor during this time so I propose that I meet you there.

Words are not enough to tell you how wonderful it will be to see my mare again. Her dam Flame Royal was an especial favourite of mine. She died a year after Wildfire was foaled.

Please acknowledge this letter and I shall make final arrangements with Miss Trevor for our meeting.

Yours sincerely,
Muriel Raynor

Jinny crouched down and picked up the photograph. She turned it over and there was Shantih. She was younger, leggier than the Shantih Jinny had always known but there could be no doubt. The photograph was of Shantih: was of Wildfire of Talisker.

Jinny sat down at her table and buried her head in her arms. Without Shantih there was nothing left in her life, and yet she was powerless to keep her. The fear and terror of what lay before her dredged through her being. It was too terrible. Could not have happened. 'Please God,' she mouthed but it was beyond being prayed for. Mrs Raynor must have prayed to find her mare again and now she had got what she wanted. Even the power of the Red Horse could not change the fact that at the end of November this unknown Mrs Raynor would come and take Shantih away. A hard, dry noise creaked in Jinny's throat. 'No,' she mouthed helplessly. 'No.'

She stayed with her face pressed hard into her arms and into the darkness came images of Shantih – Shantih high-stepping round her field, the breeze fanning out her mane and lifting her bannered tail into golden strands of light; Shantih storm-darkened, her ears laid and nostrils drawn, her quarters frost-gleaming as she had endured the winter on Finmory's moors, and Shantih bright-eyed and welcoming, at the sound of Jinny's bucket-carrying approach.

Hardly breathing, Jinny rode her mare over moorland gallops and through the translucent, sea-glimmer of Finmory Bay; felt her soar over stone walls and makeshift jumps.

And to all the delight and joy and intensity of Jinny's life with Shantih, there was to be an end. An end sealed by the day of Ardair Show.

When Jinny had been worried about the circus no one had taken her seriously, but now all her family were concerned and sympathetic. Even Ken had to agree that the photograph was Shantih.

'Try not to worry,' her father consoled her on Tuesday evening when he had read Mrs Raynor's letter. 'We'll find some way of scraping the money together. We'll buy her from Mrs Raynor.'

'A thousand pounds?' Jinny had said hopelessly. 'Probably more? No way. We could never afford it and you know we couldn't. Anyway if Shantih is the last foal of her favourite mare, it's Shantih she'll want, not money.'

'It hasn't happened yet,' said Mr Manders. 'You've weeks yet. Ardair Show isn't until the end of November.'

'I'll just forget about it all then?' said Jinny. 'Not think about it? Be the best way?'

'No need to be . . .' began her mother but checked herself. She couldn't imagine what Jinny would do without Shantih but she knew her daughter was right. They could not afford a thousand pounds. 'We'll find some way,' she said. 'Promise we will.'

'You can't promise,' said Jinny. 'You know we can't afford to buy her.'

Until the middle of the summer Mr Manders had been able to sell all the pottery he and Ken made to Nell Storr's local craft shop, but now that Nell had closed her shop and got married, a large Inverburgh store with branches throughout Scotland bought their pots. They weren't Nell. They wouldn't stockpile Manders pots for a busier season or do their best to arrange commissions for Mr Manders' pottery. If the sales dropped, Manders' income would drop too. Although Mr Manders said he was writing another book, all his family knew that he was only talking about starting. They could not even afford to pay five hundred pounds for Shantih.

'Anyway, even if we had the money, Mrs Raynor wouldn't want it. She's rich – an Arab stud, holidays in Florida. There's nothing you can do.' Jinny turned and dashed out of the room before her parents could see she was crying.

Tears blinding her, she ran down to Shantih's field. Shantih and Bramble came trotting towards her as she climbed over the gate.

'Got nothing for you,' she gulped, pushing Bramble away.

The Highland waited for a moment then realising that Jinny was speaking the truth he went back to his grazing, but Shantih stayed, sensing Jinny's distress.

'It's no use,' sobbed Jinny. 'You don't belong to me any more. She'll come and take you away and I'll never see you again. Never!' Jinny flung her arms round Shantih's neck and burying her face in Shantih's mane she cried her heart out.

'She can't, she can't,' Jinny wept. 'She can't take you away from me. I love you. You're mine. You're mine. Oh Shantih, she can't take you away.'

Then quite suddenly Jinny stopped crying. It was no use. It was going to happen. Through the darkness Jinny could hear the lonely surging of the sea in the bay. As surely as the tides would rise and fall Mrs Raynor would take Shantih away.

'No,' Jinny whispered. 'Please no,' but she had no hope.

At last she went slowly back into the house, the tears drying on her face. Now there was only an emptiness. It was as if she was living inside a transparent plastic bag. Between herself and the rest of the world there was a plastic skin. Nothing was real any longer.

'Well?' Nick said on Wednesday morning when Jinny

had told her about Mrs Raynor's letter. 'What are you going to do now? Are you going to be consumed by the vapours and the spleen of losing Shantih? Or are you going to start on your show jumping career?'

'You sound like Ken, only he isn't too keen on show jumping.'

'Come to Gavinton. It's only a potty little show. They have them every month. All ladies on ponies. Aunt Ag nearly always goes. Drums up business for herself – private lessons and liveries. Be a walkover for Shantih. Aunt Ag would pick Shantih up on the Friday before it and we could spend the weekend with them.'

'Don't know,' said Jinny. 'I'll see.'

'You are coming,' stated Nick. 'I'll tell Aunt Ag.'

Jinny neither agreed nor disagreed. She could not have cared less. Nothing mattered. She only wanted to be left alone.

'I'll tell Aunt Ag we're coming with her next Saturday,' Nick said on Friday when they were waiting for Mrs Carr to arrive and take the last class of the afternoon. 'Not tomorrow but next Saturday. Definite.'

'What?' demanded Jinny irritably.

'Gavinton. A week tomorrow. You're coming. O.K.?'

'Suppose so,' said Jinny. She didn't want to take Shantih to a show. She wanted to ride Shantih into the hills where Mrs Raynor could never find them, or to the Stopton slums where no one would ever think of looking for a lost Arab. Jinny didn't want to be part of a world where a letter from an unknown woman could take away her beloved horse.

'That's it fixed then,' said Nick. 'You'll be able to school her over your jumps this weekend.'

Jinny wasn't listening. She was thinking about going to detention after the French lesson was over; about the letter in her school bag from the headmaster to her father. She was *not* thinking about Shantih; was *not* thinking about Mrs Raynor. She was *not, not, not*.

Jinny began to tell Nick that Mr MacKenzie had padlocked the gate into the field where they had jumped, to stop Jinny doing any more damage to his ground and because of this, she wouldn't be able to practise, so really it would bc better if she didn't come.

'She rushes her jumps,' Nick went on, ignoring Jinny. 'You'll need to school her over trotting poles in front of the jump and jump only one fence instead of letting her charge round the way she does.'

'She doesn't charge round,' said Jinny indignantly. 'She is much better now.' Then she remembered that she was thinking about last Easter when, after weeks of dedicated schooling, Shantih had been settling down. But that had all been before. The plastic bag shut Jinny in again. It didn't matter.

That night, going home after detention, Jinny rode Shantih back over the mist-shrouded moors, riding slowly, letting Shantih pick her own way along the meandering sheep tracks. Sometimes she rode leaning forward with her head on one side of Shantih's neck so that she looked back upside down, at the way they had come, all her bearings lost, as Shantih carried her along. For none of it mattered. It was all no use.

Her father let her read the headmaster's letter.

'One of the schools most intelligent pupils,' 'Shows no interest in any of her work.' 'Anti social, insolent, refuses to co-operate.'

Jinny handed the letter back to her father. She had heard it all before.

'And dirty?' she suggested, and before her father could

begin to talk to her she handed the letter back to him and did an instant departure.

'You have remembered that you're coming to Aunt Ag's tomorrow?' Nick said on the following Thursday. 'That we're going to a show? You have remembered?'

Jinny didn't want to go, but not having done anything positive to stop it happening she supposed that tomorrow would bring Aunt Ag to Glenbost and Saturday would take her to Gavinton Club Show.

Jinny had spent most of the last weekend lying flat on her bed, staring at the ceiling. Her parents had nagged about acknowledging Mrs Raynor's letter and on Sunday evening Petra had written an acknowledgement, and with smug delight had announced that she would be responsible for posting it. The week had been wet, and although Jinny had jumped Shantih over a few stone walls she had made no attempt to school her. For what was the point?

'I have not forgotten,' said Jinny. 'I have even arranged my detentions so that I am free tomorrow.'

When they came out of school on Friday, Aunt Ag's horsebox was conspicuously parked in the midst of the school buses.

'Right,' said Aunt Ag as they climbed into the cab. 'Directions? I want to be home by six-thirty. Doting parents bringing their young hopeful to see a 13·2.'

Horrified, Jinny realised that Aunt Ag expected her to know the way through Inverburgh. She knew that from the school gates you went right but after that her mind was a blurr of traffic lights, roundabouts and shops. She wished wildly that Mike had been with them instead of staying for football practice. He would have known the way.

'Go right,' said Nick confidently. 'Two sets of traffic lights, then left at the Savoy cinema.'

'D'you know the way?' asked Jinny in total amazement.

'Course. This is the way the bus came when I came out to Finmory.'

'That is like a miracle to me,' Jinny said. 'Goodness knows how often I've come along here and I couldn't tell you the way to Glenbost.'

But most things about Nick were a miracle to Jinny. How could she have sold Brandon and only a fortnight later seem to have forgotten all about him, never mentioning his name? How could she be so enthusiastic about turning Shantih into a show jumper? How could she pretend that any of it mattered?

Shantih and Bramble were waiting at the field gate. Mrs Simpson was standing in her shop doorway, watching. She waved curiously to Jinny.

'Should be charging her entertainment tax, thought Jinny, going to get her case containing her riding things which she had left in the driest part of the shed.

'What's she like to box?' asked Nick, taking Shantih from Jinny as Aunt Ag lowered the ramp.

Jinny, struggling to shut in the frantic Bramble, thought of her early battles to force Shantih into a horsebox. The memory reached her through the plastic bubble that surrounded her. It had happened long ago and far away.

'O.K.,' said Jinny. 'That is sometimes. Least she's better than she used to be.'

Shantih's head was racked on a giraffe neck, her forefeet pummelled the muddy ground, her tail was at full mast– plumed and falling over her quarters, her hocks were sharp and her hind feet daggers, as she refused to approach the shaky ramp.

It began to rain, grey and constant.

Aunt Ag took Shantih's halter, turned her in tight circles

and tried to race her up the ramp, surprising Shantih into following her.

Shantih flung herself back. Her hind feet skidded in the mud and she almost fell. She stood still, shuddering.

Again and again they tried to make Shantih get into the box. To Jinny it all seemed to be happening on a television screen. She had no part in it. Could only stand in the rain, deafened by Bramble's earthshattering din, and watch as hands lifted Shantih's foreleg, placing it on the loose boards of the ramp, only to see it snatched back again the second it was freed. Wild figures shouted and waved at Shantih but she only reared away from them in panic. Obediently Jinny held the end of a rope looped round Shantih's rump. With Nick holding the other end they tried to force Shantih up the ramp, but with no success. Aunt Ag tried the lure of rustling oats in the scoop. Mrs Simpson brought apples, but nothing they did made any difference to Shantih. She spun and whirled in her total refusal to approach the box.

'Should have brought my long rope and a leather head collar,' said Aunt Ag when they stood staring in defeat at the sweating Arab. 'There's a fixed ring at the back of the box. Loop the rope through that and you can haul them in, neat as a trout. But of course now we need it I haven't got it.'

Despite the rain, Shantih was white with carded sweat.

'It doesn't matter,' said Jinny. I'll take her home. She doesn't want to go.'

'Doesn't want!' Nick raged. 'Doesn't want! And you're going to let her get away with it.'

'Then I'll ride her in,' said Jinny.

'Too dangerous,' stated Aunt Ag. 'Saw a girl try that and the horse came down with her. Broke both her legs.'

'Shantih won't fall on me,' said Jinny, hardly considering

the possibility. She had to find some way of putting an end to this ridiculous pantomime.

Aunt Ag looked at her watch. She saw it was twenty-past five and she thought about the profit she would make if she sold the 13·2 pony.

Not waiting for permission, Jinny brought Shantih's tack from the box, put it on and mounted.

'I'll ride her up and down for a bit,' she said and turned Shantih away from the dreaded box.

'Steady the horse,' she murmured. 'Gently now. What a nonsense.' As she talked she felt the fight and fear leave Shantih; felt her relax, give in and accept.

'Go into the box,' Jinny persuaded. 'The ramp is safe. It is. I'll stay with you. Nothing to be afraid of. I'll not leave you.'

But Jinny whispered with a plastic tongue. She could no longer speak a true word to Shantih. It was all lies, for soon Jinny would allow Mrs Raynor to take her away for ever.

Jinny rode Shantih back to the box, kept her walking steadily towards it. At the foot of the ramp the Arab stopped but Jinny's voice went on. The firm, gentle pressure from Jinny's seat and legs didn't change. Jinny's reins were short but her fingers held them so lightly there was no pressure on Shantih's mouth – only an insistence as constant as water, as powerful as water.

For minutes Shantih stood as if hypnotised by Jinny, then without any warning she exploded up the ramp and plunged into the box. Jinny slipped from the saddle and was at her head, praising, soothing, caressing.

'Ace,' said Nick.

'Thank the lord,' said Aunt Ag.

'I'll stay in here with her.' Despite Aunt Ag's protests, Jinny tied Shantih up and stayed beside her as the box hurtled towards Foxholm. She felt neither shame over Shantih's bad behaviour nor satisfaction with her own skill. She was only playing a part in a meaningless game.

When Jinny unloaded Shantih in Aunt Ag's yard Steph and Richard came hurrying to see her.

'Oh, isn't she gorgeous!' exclaimed Steph. 'She's a magic horse out of a fairy tale. Oh, I would love an Arab like her.'

'Flashy,' said Richard with rather less enthusiasm. 'Bet she can be a handful when she feels like it.'

'She was,' said Nick. 'She'd have climbed on to the top of the box rather than gone into it.'

'Can see that from the state she's in,' agreed Richard. 'But I really meant when you're sitting on top.'

'Not really,' said Jinny. 'Her paces are so smooth you don't notice when she's flying about. Least, I'm used to her.'

'Or it could be your riding?' suggested Richard, making Jinny glow with pride.

They ate supper of baked potatoes and stew, beseiged by Beardies.

'Really they are not allowed in the kitchen,' said Steph, 'but they love it so. You can't keep them shut out all the time.'

'I could,' said Richard, picking a Beardie hair out of his plate.

He was coming to Gavinton with them, bringing Midas, the black horse he was schooling, and entering him in the Handy Horse competition, so that Midas's owner would see that he was getting value for money.

'Take Meg,' said Steph, as Nick and Jinny went out to groom Shantih. 'She so hates it when all that mob break in.'

In the dim, stable light, Nick, with her arms round Meg sat watching Jinny grooming Shantih. The Arab was uneasy, ears flickering to the threat of the strange stable. She swung away from Jinny to circle the box. With sharp, querulous neighs she called for Bramble and lifted a fretful hoof to strike the concrete floor with her metal shoe.

Gradually, under the soothing strokes of the body brush, Shantih settled to her haynet. Meg closed her eyes and slept, chin on Nick's knee.

'What did your mother say when you gave her the cheque?' Jinny asked suddenly, the question in her mind turned into words before she had really known she was going to ask it. 'Was she pleased?'

Nick looked up, startled. Since Brandon had been sold she hadn't mentioned money to Jinny.

'Guilty,' she said. 'Did the whole bit – tears and clutching and telling me how she would make it up to me. But she wasn't pleased. She hates me for it. Making her feel so rotten guilty.'

Next morning sky and earth were masked by pouring rain. A steady downpour that might go on for weeks, would certainly go on all day.

Jinny woke to the sound of the rain drumming on the roof and longed to turn over and go to sleep again. She did not want to go to Gavinton, did not want to fight Shantih into the horsebox again; more than anything did not want to get up, for to get up was to go to bed again and that meant that another of her few precious days with Shantih would have been squandered.

Richard boxed the black Midas first, rushing him in through the downpour. Then Steph loaded Sparkle, her black pony.

'You're going home,' Jinny lied to Shantih, but it did not matter for everything was lies now; all false. 'Going back to Bramble.'

Jinny walked confidently towards the ramp. Sparkle whinnied and Shantih seeing the black pony already in the box sprang up the ramp with one leap. Richard was behind her and as Jinny tied Shantih to the side of the box, he squared her up and fitted a partition between Shantih and the ramp.

'That's her,' Richard said checking that Jinny had tied Shantih up with a quick release knot. 'No bother this time. Now let's get a move on. I'm riding that twit in the Handy Horse and that's the second class.'

'Got everything?' Aunt Ag checked when they were all squashed in the cabin beside her. 'Hard hats, boots, tack? Too late once we get there. O.K.?'

The engine spluttered, coughed and died.

'Oh no!' cried Richard. 'Not this again!'

Aunt Ag pulled the starter and pumped pedals. Richard did the same. But in the end Uncle Christy had to be dragged out to burrow in the engine before the box condescended to move.

'Arriving late so I miss the class. They'll think we're doing it on purpose,' Richard said.

'They never start on time,' cheered Aunt Ag, her foot hard down on the accelerator. 'We'll make it.'

Last Easter, Jinny had ridden in a cross country competition at Brandoch Country Club. She had been expecting Gavinton Country Club to be something the same – flat paddocks fenced with white posts and rails, a cross country course, large car parks and the Club itself a country house with modern extensions. As the float turned up the lane that led to Gavinton Jinny saw it was not going to be at all the same.

The grey stone house was run down; the fields surrounding it rough and uncared for; the scant hedges were reinforced with stobs, wire, and planks of wood. Jinny could see no sign of any show jumping ring.

'Where is it held?'

'Other side of the house,' said Nick as the wheels of the box spun and skidded over the muddy ground.

But even when Aunt Ag had driven the box to the other side of the Club and parked it with the other floats and trailers, Jinny could still see no sign of show jumps. A few riders wearing oilskins were riding their horses in a small paddock which seemed to be nothing but a sea of mud.

'As I feared,' said Richard. 'We will be in the sardine tin.'

'It's inside,' explained Nick. 'Too wet and too churned up out here.'

As they all piled out of the cabin and ran into the Club it gradually began to dawn on Jinny, inside her isolating plastic skin, that Shantih had never been ridden in an indoor school before. Jinny thought vaguely that Shantih might not like it.

Sitting on Shantih some three hours later, Jinny was still thinking the same thing. With four other horses she was waiting in a tiny roped-in corner of the school which was referred to as the collecting ring. The class was for horses over 14·2 hands. There was no restriction on the riders' ages. Most of the other riders were much older than Jinny.

Gavinton indoor school was as Richard had said, terrifyingly small. There was a row of four pillars down the middle of the tan, a spectator gallery at one end and arranged in the limited space were the jumps. Perched on Shantih's tight back Jinny felt as if she were a spectator. She hardly knew what she was doing there.

'Well, look who's here! You're the redhead who was with Nick Webster when the Old Man bought her horse for me. You're not really going to jump that little tick, are you? I knew Gavinton was the bottom but show jumping an Arab!'

Jinny looked round to see Liam Orme pushing his way into the collecting ring astride a young, dapple grey. As he spoke he leaned forward and tapped Shantih on the quarters with his riding stick.

Hemmed in tightly by four other horses, Shantih exploded vertically. Her back humped as she leapt like a rodeo horse. Twisting and shaking her neck, she struck out with her hind feet and then, rearing, lashed out in front. Somehow Jinny stayed on top; somehow she managed to gather in her reins; somehow sat out the explosion until Nick, bulleting to her side, grabbed Shantih's bit ring and brought her under control again.

'You idiot!' cried Jinny, turning on Liam. 'You stupid, crazy fool! What a stupid thing to do.'

Liam was leaning back in his saddle helpless with laughter; his legs stuck forward; his mouth wide as he roared with delight.

'Want another little tickle?' he gasped.

'Don't you dare touch her,' yelled Jinny. 'Leave her alone.'

'If you annoy that girl's horse again I'll go straight to a steward,' warned a woman who had narrowly missed being kicked by Shantih. 'You should be disqualified for that.'

The woman in the ring rode out, Liam's number was called, and digging his heels into the grey's sides he forced his way through the other riders in the collecting ring.

Liam grinned as he rode past Jinny, shaking his stick at her.

He rode a clear round – sitting solid in the saddle, beating his horse into the fences and sitting upright as she jumped.

His fists on the reins, hauled at her mouth, yanking her round the course.

Shantih waited – eyes goggling, tight and tense. Nick turned away and Jinny knew that she saw Liam riding, not the grey, but Brandon. Froth splattered the grey's face as Liam trotted her out of the ring.

Jinny's number was called and as Shantih burst out of the collecting ring Liam flicked her with his stick. In the gallery someone let off a flash bulb and Shantih screamed a high, piercing neigh that chilled Jinny's blood.

'Stop it! Calm down,' she cried but her voice was tense and shrill. The glare of the electric light was menacing and harsh. The tan beneath Shantih's hooves felt strange, 'Oh Shantih, steady. Steady,' she cried.

Shantih charged the first jump and leapt crazily over it. Her head outstretched, neck low she went like a tornado for the next post and rails, then she was over it and stampeding on at the double.

Remote and cold, Jinny clung to Shantih's mane. She had no control over this whirlwind, this explosion of energy. Jostled and shaken she could only endure. Yet even the endurance, the shame was happening to someone else. Jinny wasn't really there in the ring at Gavinton. She was waiting at Finmory for the sound of Mrs Raynor's horse-box.

Shantih skidded round the last pillar, a fraction closer and she would have shattered Jinny's knee against it. Tight and furious and mad she flung herself at the first part of a double, touched down and rose again to land in the middle of the second part. Poles crashed and splintered around Jinny. One caught in Shantih's hindlegs and sent her sprawling to the ground. A spectator screamed as Shantih skidded along on her belly before she surged upright and, with Jinny still in the saddle, thundered back to the collecting ring.

Nick grabbed at Shantih's rein and dragged her to a halt. Strangers crowded round wanting to know whether Jinny was all right, while Liam Orme leant back against his grey's shoulder, blurting with laughter, tears running from his eyes.

'It was you!' Jinny yelled at him. 'You! All your fault. That's right, go on laugh. She could have broken her back and all you can do is laugh!'

Jinny's fury tore her free from her plastic covering. She was fully alive again. Furious and suffering that Shantih should have made such an exhibition of herself when it was all Liam Orme's fault.

'My fault?' spluttered Liam 'Go home, cowboy and learn to ride. And before you come back buy yourself a horse, not that fairy!'

Jinny rode Shantih past him, out into the grey rain of the afternoon. She dropped from the saddle and faced Nick across Shantih's back.

'Wait until Ardair Show,' she swore. 'Let him bloomin' well wait and I'll show him whether Shantih can jump or not!'

CHAPTER NINE

'Well?' said Mr Manders as Jinny laid the forms to register Shantih with the British Show Jumping Association, and herself as a Junior Associate Member, in front of him.

'You have only to sign. Aunt Ag's filled the rest in. You have to join as a Non-jumping Member, so you can register Shantih.'

'And pay,' said Mr Manders when he had read through the documents.

'Not too terribly much.'

'What are you trying to do? This won't stop Mrs Raynor coming to see Shantih.'

'Never thought it would,' said Jinny. 'It's got nothing to do with her. I want to prove that Shantih can show jump. Nick is sure she's good enough. And because Mrs Raynor's coming to take her away I've got to do it now or it will be too late.'

'You've been listening to Nick, filling your head with her ambitions.'

'I have not. It's not like that a bit. It's for Shantih. I want to win for her. Show them what she can really do after the muck-up at Gavinton. One last thing before she has to go.'

The blaze and dazzle of jumping at Ardair Show blinded out all thoughts of Mrs Raynor. It let Jinny say, "because Mrs Raynor's coming to take her away', without thinking about it; without suffering it. She could lie in bed at night, her head filled with thoughts of show jumping, or sit at the back of the Maths class dreaming of spread jumps, brush fences and walls solid as houses. The disaster of Gavinton was behind her. In her dreams, Shantih jumped in the ring as she did at home – flying the jumps, soaring, leaping for delight.

'Please sign them. They must be posted as soon as possible.'

'I'll make a deal with you,' said Mr Manders, putting the forms down and looking straight at Jinny. 'I sign these and pay. You are in the top ten in the exams.'

Last term Jinny had been twenty-sixth in her class of thirty. Only her Art mark had stopped her from being bottom.

'Oh Dad!'

'Your headmaster thinks you could be. So how about it? Your word that you'll do it. Obviously if I sign these and pay, you could go off and forget all about it, say you tried and couldn't do any better but I want your word that you will be in the top ten. Not trying, not doing your best, but changing so that you're where you should be.'

'I won't have time! I'll have to school Shantih like mad. Nick's got a time-table all worked out.'

'All you need to do is work while you are at school.'

Jinny shut her eyes and groaned from her depths.

'Sign,' she said.

For the first lesson next morning, Jinny sat down at the front of the class.

'I'm sitting at the front from now on,' she told Nick and Dolina, giving Nick the completed registration forms and her father's cheque. 'I've got to be top this term.'

'Sez who?' asked Mac Brown, the boy who was always top and always sat in the front row.

'Sez me,' Jinny replied. 'I've got to improve so I may as well be top.'

Nick said the most important thing was to steady Shantih, to stop her associating jumping with full out galloping.

'She's got the ability,' said Nick. 'No doubt about that. We've got to give her confidence in jumping small obstacles calmly. Trotting poles four and a half feet apart. Jump one small spread jump, never a course. Use half halts when you land, not pulling on your reins and try a pole about two feet away on the landing side of the jump to stop her rushing off.'

Every day after school Jinny worked on Shantih. She rode circles at the sitting trot and slow canter. She set up one spread fence of about two feet which she jumped from a trot, steadying Shantih with her voice and half halts, bringing her back to a trot and circling her, refusing to let her dash off wildly after jumping.

The first few afternoons Jinny tried to cope with the trotting poles herself. Laying them out at what she thought was the correct distance apart in front of the jump, then mounting and riding over them. But this meant that when Shantih kicked one out of place Jinny had to dismount to put it back. Horrified at the sight of a pole being dragged along the ground Shantih would spring away and whirl madly round, doing her best to stop Jinny remounting and all Jinny's calm schooling would be disrupted.

She had chosen the best of the poles from Mr MacKenzie's field and brought them up to the Finmory field which meant that screams from Bramble in his box was another source of constant disturbance. Then she had the bright idea of bribing Mike into being her assistant.

'I'll do all your maps and anything else you have to draw for the rest of this term, if you'll help me school Shantih. Set up poles and jumps and that sort of thing. I have to school her every night, so even if it's pouring you'll have to be there to help me.'

'What about the nights you're in detention?'

'No more,' said Jinny. 'I've given up detention for good.'

'Do my maps until Easter and some drawings for my Social Studies project,' bargained Mike and Jinny accepted.

Mike's eye turned out to be better than Jinny's. When he had watched her riding over the trotting poles one or two times he suggested that they were too close together.

'She almost clips them everytime. Wait and I'll make them a bit further apart.'

When Mike had changed the poles Jinny rode over them again and immediately she could feel the difference. Now Shantih's trot swung through her back with a strong rythmn. When she came to the last pole which was a foot high the distance was exactly right for her to jump neatly over it.

Pleased with his success, Mike borrowed a book on Equitation from the Inverburgh Library. He studied it with Jinny and then wheedled some better poles from Mr MacKenzie, borrowed his mother's tape-measure and set up various grids for Shantih to jump. He varied them from simple trotting poles with various distances between the last pole and the small jump. He set up two small fences with either one or two strides between them at the end of the trotting grid.

At the end of the first week after Gavinton Jinny thought Shantih was improving. By the next weekend, when Nick came to inspect their progress, Shantih was jumping three small fences set in the schooling circle; jumping them from a trot without any excitement. She neither raced coming in to them, nor charged off after jumping them. Nick was impressed.

'Try a canter round,' she said. 'Wait till I put them up. If you canter her over these she'll only take them in her stride and flatten her back. I'll put them up to three feet. We want her to go on basculing – arching – over them.'

Shantih cantered smoothly over them.

'Nice,' praised Nick. 'You've not only been working at school.'

For a moment, flushed with success, Jinny forgot about Mrs Raynor; forgot that all her desire to make Shantih into a show jumper was only a cover-up story to hide the truth from herself.

On Sunday morning they went for a ride over the moors, and to Jinny's satisfaction Shantih stayed supple and obedient. No longer did she bound into a tearaway gallop at every opportunity. She arched accurately over stone walls, no longer soaring feet above them.

Nick was no longer merely impressed, she was envious.

'If she goes on improving like this,' she said, 'and still jumps the heights she can clear when she's berserking about, she's going to be rather good.'

'Take the Talisker Stud by storm?'

Richard came in the afternoon and gave Shantih a blanket clip. To everyone's surprise, Shantih, bribed with peppermint chocolate creams, stood staring into the middle distance while Richard's clippers furrowed their way through soft falls of chestnut hair.

Aunt Ag had lent Jinny a stable rug and a New Zealand rug. The New Zealand rug was slightly too big for Shantih. Turned out in it, she looked waifish and woebegone as she watched them, her clipped face naked.

A lump choked in Jinny's throat. What had she done, turning Shantih into this miserable creature who had to be wrapped up to survive?

'Forgive us our sins,' Ken said when he saw her but Richard said Jinny would be able to work the mare now. Get her fit. Put some muscle on her.

Jinny listened to Richard not to Ken. It was Richard's world that Jinny was holding on to. Richard's world where danger was balanced against excitement; where cups and rosettes were to be won and held and where winning mattered.

Now that Shantih was clipped and stabled at night, Jinny had to get up early to feed and water her before she had her own breakfast. After breakfast, eaten with only Kelly to keep her company, she went back to the stable, took a brush over Shantih and set off for Glenbost. With plenty of time to spare, Jinny sometimes schooled by herself in the field by Mrs Simpson's shop or rode Shantih on to Ardtallon and back again. Jinny rode with all her attention fixed on her horse, not staring about her, lost in a dream world. She made Shantih walk out with an even, unhurried stride; changing from a sitting trot to a rising trot and back to a sitting trot; all the time using her seat and legs to create impulsion.

In the evenings Jinny left the New Zealand rug with Mrs Simpson and rode Shantih home over the moors, cantering her up and downhill as she always had done, popping her over dry stone walls for the fun of it. Then, with Mike to help, she schooled her over poles and grids for a short while in the Finmory field. As the days grew shorter Mr Manders moved the poles to the Glenbost field so that Jinny could make the most of the light, and jump Shantih there.

Every weekend Nick came to stay to help Jinny with Shantih and to check up on their progress. Every weekend that was seven days nearer to Ardair Show. Time through an hourglass that would not stop for the least pico second, yet ran faster and faster as the weeks passed.

Mr Manders had not been pleased at Shantih having to be brought in at night so soon.

'It's to get her fit,' said Jinny. 'So I can feed her more.'

'That's what I'm saying,' said her father.

'It's all part of our bargain. No point in joining the BSJA if I haven't got a fit horse to compete on.'

'And your side of the bargain?'

'Ev-i-dence,' croaked Jinny, computering the facts. 'Pro-gress re-port on Manders J. Was top in last French translation test. On throwing Arithmetic excercise book back at Manders J. Mr Palmer was heard to exclaim that he could not believe it possible – ten out of ten for Arithmetic homework. Eighteen out of twenty for last English essay. Teacher's comment – 'Is this your own work?' Ple-ease ack-know-ledge if re-port sat-is-fac-tory.'

'Ack-know-ledge tot-al sat-is-fact-ion.'

'Would also like to point out that equine consumer will not be eating with us for much longer.'

'You're kidding no one,' said Mike. 'We all know how miserable it must be for you. But you won't let us help you. Won't even talk about it!'

'That-is-how-it-is,' computered Jinny.

'If Mrs Raynor can prove that Shantih used to belong to her, then we'll find out what can be done,' Mr Manders said kindly, but to Jinny he only sounded adult and disinterested and offered her no hope.

'You won't meet Mrs Raynor. She will claim Wildfire at Ardair Show and you won't be there.'

'Of course we'll come to Ardair,' said Mr Manders. 'Got to give you our support. Can't let you cope with Mrs Raynor without us on your side.'

'Sup-port is not re-quired.'

'Oh Jinny!'

'There's nothing you can do, so there's no point in you trailing to Ardair.' And Jinny had departed to groom Shantih.

Every night she spent an hour strapping her. Thwacking the rubber down on to Shantih's shoulders and quarters and neck, reciting French verbs or science experiments as she did so.

'Don't suppose there will be too many moors for you to gallop over in Dorset,' Jinny told her. 'Though I dare say it will be posh. When they've taken you away will you dream of Finmory?'

Catching the emotion in Jinny's voice Shantih turned her primped, clipped face to look at her. Her eyes were enormous, the dark patches around them – called in Arabs "painted skin" – gave her the face of a golden unicorn, half doe, half horse but with a wild, fey magic beyond both of them.

'Don't cry,' Jinny warned herself. 'What is there to cry for? I will be jumping Shantih in a Real Show.' But tears stung in her eyes and the lines of white light on Shantih's gleaming coat flashed into diamonds.

From the second Jinny opened her eyes in the morning to the second she shut them at night she never had a spare moment, never had time to think.

Now she had started working at school, lessons were no longer boring. In one incredible Algebra lesson Jinny actually understood equations. She saw quite clearly the dance of the figures, as precise and formal as a dressage test. The teachers who had never approved of her prophesied that the change couldn't last, but those who liked her said they had always known she could do well if she would only pay attention, and now she was.

'Richard has found an indoor school,' Nick told Jinny on the Wednesday morning before Ardair Show.

'Where?' asked Jinny.

'Mr Young's.'

From the beginning Nick had been keen to find an indoor school where they could jump Shantih before Ardair.

'I know Liam annoyed her at Gavinton but it might have been the lights and the tan as well. It was all too sudden for her. Mind you, she is much better schooled now, but seeing that Richard has tracked down Mr Young's, it's a super chance.'

'You might see Brandon?'

'So what? I shan't mind.' Nick spoke as if being sentimental over Brandon was the most ridiculous idea in the world. 'He's sold. That's that. Don't even know if Liam keeps him there.'

In three days Shantih would have gone too. If not actually taken away, a time would have been arranged for Mrs Raynor to collect her. It was so unthinkable, so terrible, that Jinny had shut it out of her life. Even the night before, when Miss Trevor had phoned leaving a message with Mike to tell them that Mrs Raynor had arrived back safely from Florida and would be at Ardair Show on Saturday afternoon, Jinny still couldn't bring herself to talk about it to anyone.

'When are we going to Mr Young's?' she asked Nick.

'Do you think you could dog an afternoon off on Friday? Aunt Ag could pick you up at Finmory. Richard fixed it up for Friday afternoon. He's going to give Warrior a school as well.'

'I think,' said Jinny, 'I could do better than that. Mr Lawson told me on Monday to tell my father that he was exceptionally, note well *exceptionally*, pleased with my all round improvement. I haven't mentioned it yet, so I reckon I could trade that in for a day off.'

Mr Manders did not quite see the connection but in the end he allowed himself to be persuaded.

'Only this once,' he said. 'It is not a precedent.'

'There won't be another time.'

'Sit down,' said her father, 'and let's discuss Shantih. You won't talk about it so how can we help you? If Mrs Raynor could prove that Shantih belongs to her then she will need to come here and see me about it.'

'What's the point? Shantih is Wildfire. The photograph was Shantih and that's all there is to it. You can tell from her letters how desperate she is to have her back; how much she's missed her. If Mrs Raynor has a horsebox with her she may as well take her away on Saturday. Get it over with.'

'Oh Jinny! She will not be taking her away on Saturday.'

'Nothing to stop her,' said Jinny, but even in her own ears her attempt to copy Nick sounded pathetically phoney.

Aunt Ag arrived at twelve on Friday, bringing her long rope and head collar with her. Jinny had spent the last of the money she had earned from selling her drawings to Nell Storr, on yellow bandages for Shantih. When Jinny led her up to the horsebox, rugged and bandaged, she looked every inch a show jumper.

As Aunt Ag was putting the headcollar on Shantih she sprang away from her and, catching Aunt Ag off balance, broke free and went bucking away over the garden.

'Doesn't want to come,' said Aunt Ag. 'Strange how animals know.'

Jinny went to catch her. She held out her hand with a squashed fruit pastille on it. As Shantih came up to her, walking warily, yet trusting Jinny, it was almost too much. Jinny's hand shook and her lips trembled.

'Don't bloomin' well cry,' she told herself. 'Don't let them see you crying. If you start making a scene now, it's all wasted. You needn't have bothered. Might as well have spent your time riding her on the moors. All that schooling was to stop this happening. You're a show jumper now. Your horse is registered with the BSJA. Tomorrow you're jumping in the Pathfinder competition and the Topscore competition. Tomorrow you're going to win.'

Shantih took the fruit pastille, her lips brushing Jinny's palm and Jinny dropped the rope over her outstretched neck.

'Well held,' cheered Aunt Ag as Jinny led Shantih back to her. 'Now this time let's get her in.'

Held by the rope through the ring on the cavesson which was looped through the fixed ring at the back of the box, Shantih was slowly but surely drawn into the box. And the image of her horse, so smart in her bright yellow bandages and rug, her delicate clipped face stretched unnaturally in front of her by the rope, being forced to leave Finmory, was branded on Jinny's memory.

Mrs Manders handed up Jinny's case of cleaned and pressed riding clothes, then her jacket and boots.

'Do well,' said her mother. 'And remember, We are coming to the show to help you cope with Mrs Raynor. So stop torturing yourself.'

'No point,' Jinny replied, but her voice broke and she had to look quickly away from her mother and was glad when Aunt Ag created a distraction by climbing up into the cab.

When they reached Mr Young's, Richard, mounted on Warrior, was waiting in the yard and Nick, standing beside him, was talking to Mr Young.

'Very kind of you,' Aunt Ag said. 'Forgot you had the old barn.'

'It does, it does,' said Mr Young. 'Not five star but then what is these days?'

Nick helped Jinny to unload Shantih. She burst wide-eyed from the box and refused to stand while Jinny, wishing she had not bothered, tried to untie her bandages.

'So this is the demolition expert,' Mr Young said. 'Heard a few reports. I don't charge for the use of my school but anything broken has to be replaced. Understood?' He fixed Jinny with his bead-bright eyes.

Jinny said she understood, remembering too late that of course you didn't untie tail bandages, you pulled them off.

At last, after a moment of blind panic, when she was certain she had left her hard hat behind, she mounted and followed Richard down a narrow passage between two outbuildings.

The doors of the large barn were wide open and Mr Young had switched on the lights. The low corrugated roof curved over a floor of tan and dung. Ponies obviously used it as a shelter. Eight jumps were set up, all about three feet six to four feet.

'Better school first,' Richard said, smiling his toothpaste-ad smile at Jinny.

Shantih lifted her feet high from the soft ground. She advanced down the school in a series of caprioles, pig squealing from her wide nostrils.

'Let her go forward,' Nick shouted. 'Sitting trot. Push her on.'

Jinny, fearing a repeat of Gavinton, did as she was told. By the time she had circled the school twice, Shantih was back on her bit, her rythmn established, she listened to her rider. Jinny worked her in circles, concentrating on changing her paces. All her work had been worth it. Shantih was a different horse now to the mad mare who had crashed her way round the ring at Gavinton. For a forgetful minute Jinny felt a glow of pride at her own achievement and then she remembered – she was riding Wildfire.

'If we're here to jump, let's get on with it,' Richard called. 'I'll go first.' He urged Warrior into a canter and rode him at the first jump – an upright post and rails.

Warrior jumped big. In the confines of the school he looked to Jinny as if he might jump through the tin roof. Suddenly the jumps looked huge to her and she wondered if Shantih would be able to clear them. Jinny had never thought this about Shantih before but for the past weeks she had been jumping no more than three feet so as not to overface her. Tomorrow, competing in Pathfinder and Topscore competitions as a Junior Associate, she would be riding against adults. The jumps would be big then, as well.

'Your turn,' said Richard, pulling Warrior to a halt.

'Jump her down the left hand side first,' Nick told Jinny. 'Then trot her back up the middle. Go down the far side of the jumps and round at the bottom and jump back up on the other side.'

Jinny nodded, cantered Shantih in a circle and, concentrating her total energy on her horse and her riding, she took her over the four jumps. Balanced and confident, Shantih cleared them. She landed and cantered on without any attempt to charge at the next jump. At the far end of the school she turned when Jinny asked her to, trotted straight up to the open doors, down the far side and round, to jump her way back up. After the last jump – an upright white gate with no wings – she came sweetly back to hand.

Nick and Jinny gazed at each other in wordless triumph.

'Well, well,' smiled Richard. 'Cousin Nick has the touch.'

'All Jinny,' said Nick.

'Wait until tomorrow night,' Jinny warned, as Richard took Warrior round again.

'O.K.?' Richard was asking, 'satisfied?' when they heard the sound of trotting hoofs coming towards them along the narrow way that led from the yard to the school.

'Next booking?' wondered Richard as Liam came out of the passage and rode towards them. The pony he was riding was white with sweat. It's hooves pounded the ground as it fought Liam to get to the jumps. Its head was strapped down with a short standing martingale attached to a drop noseband. He held the reins of a twisted snaffle in one hand leaving the other free for his whip.

Jinny heard Nick gasp with a hardly audible sound and at once she realised that the pony Liam was riding was Brandon.

'Have you seen Mr Young?' Liam shouted.

'No. He's not here,' Richard replied.

'Great! I'll get a school round without him interfering.' Liam rode Brandon into the school before he recognised them.

'Well,' he cried. 'If it isn't Little Miss Tickle Tantrum. Here for another little tickle?'

Richard on Warrior, towering above Liam, rode quickly in front of Jinny.

'Leave Jinny alone,' he warned. 'If you even speak to her again like that I'll put you into next week. Understood?'

'Only a laugh,' said Liam. 'Just a joke. No need to come on the heavy.'

'Understood?' demanded Richard again.

Liam pulled Brandon out of Richard's way. His fist, clenched on the reins, was level with Brandon's ears. The long cutting whip flickered against Brandon's side as he swung him away.

Brandon's eyes screamed silently; his ears were pinned to his neck; his mouth was held shut by the drop noseband as he fought to free his head from the restraint of the martingale. Nick stood staring at him. Never taking her eyes off Brandon.

'What has he done,' Jinny thought wildly, 'to turn Nick's willing pony into this frenzied lunatic.'

'He's jumping like a bomb,' Liam said. 'Told you I'd waken him up. You'll see, we'll be in the money tomorrow as long as the ancient keeps his nose out of the way. Want to see me jump before he comes interfering?'

Nick turned her back on Liam and walked out of the indoor school.

'If that scab bothers you again, let me know,' Richard said.

'Will do,' said Jinny.

'He's ruined Brandon,' Richard said. 'Drop noseband with a martingale attached to it. At least he can't put that on him in the ring.'

'They bought him,' said Nick. 'They can do what they like with him.'

Nick's voice was firm and clear. Her face showed no sign of emotion, so that even Jinny couldn't tell whether she meant what she said or not.

CHAPTER TEN

Jinny woke to the early dark of a winter morning and the sound of Nick's voice telling her it was time to get up. At first she couldn't even remember where she was and then the day to be swept over her. She pulled the bedclothes over her head and curled up tightly. She hardly knew which was the more terrifying, the thought of meeting Mrs Raynor or the thought of show jumping Shantih. Desperately she did not want either to happen. Jinny wanted to stay where she was, safe and secure.

'Come on. Up,' insisted Nick.

'Am doing,' said Jinny, but she was not.

She did not really think that Mrs Raynor would have a horsebox with her. Not when she had just flown back from Florida, not when she was under doctor's orders, but she was sure that Shantih was Wildfire of Talisker; that Mrs Raynor would know her at once and would make arrangements for her to be returned to her stud. That today was her last day when Shantih was Shantih.

'What am I doing?' Jinny thought. 'Taking Shantih to meet her. Why didn't I try and find some way of hiding Shantih. That's what I should have been doing, not show jumping!'

At that moment Jinny couldn't think of anything more ridiculous than trying to turn Shantih into a show jumper. With a shuddering clarity she remembered Gavinton.

'Up,' commanded Nick and seizing Jinny's bedclothes she stripped them off her and left her exposed to the arctic temperature of the bedroom.

With Warrior, Sparkle and Shantih swaying and propping to the movement of the box, Aunt Ag drove through the brightening morning towards Ardair.

'Last year Brandon won two red rosettes,' said Steph.

'Probably will again this year,' Nick said. 'Liam thinks he will.'

'We've to jump in the outdoor ring,' Steph grumbled. 'It's not a bit fair.'

'Lovely day for you,' said her mother.

'Wish I was jumping outside,' said Richard. 'Ardair's a good bit bigger than Gavinton but it is not vast.'

But to Jinny's eyes everything about Ardair was vast. Vaster than vast. In her wildest imagings she had never dreamed it would be so professional.

Driving in, they unloaded horses and tack into three boxes in rows of temporary stabling and Aunt Ag drove the box away to park it.

'Pathfinder is your first class,' said Nick. 'Not until eleven-thirty. Tie up Shantih's haynet and we can have a look round. You've plenty of time.'

'I can't leave her,' stated Jinny. Shantih was the one sane, familiar being in all this folly. She had to stay with her. Never leave her. Jinny had never felt less like jumping in all her life.

'Richard will watch her and Aunt Ag will be back in a moment,' Nick assured her, and grabbing Jinny's hand she dragged her away from the box. 'Half the fun seeing everything,' said Nick, but Jinny could only hear Shantih's despairing whinny following her as Nick urged her on.

Although it was only nine o'clock there was already a class jumping in the outdoor ring, and a milling of horses waiting for their turn over the practice jump. The man who was jumping it was strangely familiar. At first Jinny couldn't place him and then she recognised him as Kevin Bowes, a famous show jumper.

'I haven't woken up,' she thought. 'Jumping at the same show as Kevin Bowes!'

'Come on,' said Nick. 'Let's take a look at the jumps.'

She was bright with excitement, dancing at Jinny's side, greedily gulping in horses and riders; loving the hard-bitten faces, the strain and thud of horses cantering past, boots angled against stirrup irons, sticks rebounding from fit muscle, hands strong on reins, voices of horses and humans raised in greeting.

A steward tried to stop them going in to the arena but Nick shouted, 'Competitors,' and marched in with Jinny running behind her.

A spattering of spectators sat about the ringside. In the higher, tiered seating people were already settling in for the day – families with picnic baskets, couples watching intently, people sitting alone, studying their programmes. Under the floodlights a grey horse ridden by a tall man was gathering faults as his horse kicked off top bars.

Stricken with terror, Jinny stared at the jumps. They were enormous – mountainous spreads, stacked poles and rails and an upright white gate that seemed to Jinny's dilating eye, higher and less inviting than any jump she had ever seen. She knew with total certainty that she was here to make a fool of herself. But that didn't matter. It was making an exhibition of Shantih that mattered. Again, in the strange surroundings, in the bright and shadowed world of the indoor arena, Shantih would panic. As if it were happening now, Jinny heard the crashing of the jumps that were surely too high for Shantih to clear. These jumps were for the stars of show jumping, only to be reached by years of experience. They were not for Jinny and Shantih after their few weeks of amateurish schooling.

'They're far too high!' Jinny cried. 'Far bigger than anything we ever jumped at Finmory!'

Nick turned scornful eyes on her but it was Liam Orme's voice that answered.

'Oh dear,' he mocked. 'Little Miss Tickle got cold feet?'

Without Jinny seeing him he had come up to stand behind them.

'Mind your own business,' snapped Nick. 'And leave us alone.' She grabbed Jinny by the arm and pushed her way past Liam and out into the collecting ring.

'Really,' persisted Jinny. 'Those jumps are far too high for us.'

'Belt up!' exploded Nick. 'Those aren't the jumps for the Pathfinder comp. They'll only be a mingey three and a half feet. For goodness sake, you've jumped that on Shantih often enough.'

But Nick's scorn made no difference to Jinny. She didn't know what she was doing there. These people were not her people. They were all too hard, too forceful – single minded in their will to win. Their horses were trained for one thing only, to leap like automata, over higher and higher obstacles. Ken would have had nothing to do with them.

The mural of the Red Horse came clear into her mind and Jinny saw that he stood far off, remote from this turmoil of greed and illusion. Everything here was false. The horses perverted from their true beings. The humans as blind as Jinny had been for the past few weeks.

'I'm going back to Shantih,' Jinny said.

'Yes, better start and ride her in. Expect she'll take a while to settle. Better have a look at the course plan first.'

'I'm not going . . .' Jinny began but Nick was hurrying across to where the course plans were pinned up on a notice board. She pointed to the course plan for the Pathfinders competition. A black line linked the jumps on the diagram. Nick traced it with her finger, naming the jumps as she came to them – spread, brush, parallel poles, double.

Jinny wasn't even trying to listen. One glance at the plan had been enough. The line did not go neatly along the sides of the arena. It looped and twisted and Jinny knew with total certainty that she would never be able to remember the course when she was in the ring.

As they went back to the horses Jinny heard Shantih's whinny. She was able to pick it out at once, quite distinct from all the other noise.

Aunt Ag was waiting for them, talking to a friend who was also the mother of horse-mad children. She had already dispatched Steph, correctly numbered, to the outdoor ring.

'You're tenth to jump in Pathfinders,' she told Jinny, giving her her number. Your class starts in an hour so you'd better get Shantih underway. There's a draw for the jumping order for Topscore but that's not until this afternoon. No need to worry about that yet.'

'Afternoon,' thought Jinny as she took a body brush over Shantih in a final dusting of perfection and began to tack her up. By the afternoon Mrs Raynor would have arrived and the long drawn out misery of the past weeks would be reaching its end. Jinny would agree with her, saying, yes, Shantih was Wildfire, was exactly the same as Mrs Raynor's photographs; would be polite, saying how glad she was that Mrs Raynor had found her horse again; would listen while Mrs Raynor discussed arrangements to take Shantih back to Dorset.

'Why am I here?' thought Jinny desperately. 'What am I doing here when I should be at Finmory, riding to Loch Varrich for a last time? Not making an idiot of you here.'

As Jinny rode Shantih about the collecting ring she was conscious of other riders turning to stare at the flaunting Arab, commenting on Shantih as she fretted and danced, but Jinny paid no attention to them. She was frozen with fear.

Nick held Shantih while Jinny walked the course. Following close behind a group of loud, confident riders, Jinny had no idea what she was meant to be doing. If Nick said the jumps were lower than other obstacles that Shantih had jumped Jinny supposed they must be, but to her they looked enormous, reared up to the sky, were not to be cleared by any mortal horse. The floodlit arena was a setting for a nightmare and Jinny walked round it as detatched from reality as if she really were asleep.

'What is wrong with you?' Nick demanded. 'All the work we've put into training Shantih and now you've packed it all in! Sitting there like a zombie! What is wrong?'

'Nothing,' said Jinny. 'I didn't know it was going to be like this, that's all.'

'Like what? I thought you wanted to jump in a big show? That's what you said. And anyway this isn't all that big. It's not bloomin' Wembley!'

Liam rode past, kicking Brandon on while his fixed hands held him back. The little horse was tight as a coiled spring. His plunging hocks drove energy into his forehand and Liam drew it back through the bit, along the reins into his hands. Held the power in to himself. He was not jumping until later and ignored Jinny and Nick completely.

'I don't know,' said Nick furiously. 'Here you are with a super horse who can jump far higher than any of the jumps in there and you've packed it in. While I have to stand here and watch that bully-basher ruining Brandon.'

Jinny felt neither sympathy for Nick nor fury at Liam. She waited. She did not want to have to ride Shantih into the ring. Did not want to have to cling to her, helplessly out of control, while Shantih crashed her way through the jumps. But she could see no way of avoiding it.

A steward called her number and without a glance at Nick, Jinny rode Shantih into the smaller space between the collecting ring and the arena. The main entrance to the arena ran by the side of where Jinny waited. It was busier now as a constant stream of spectators made their way to their seats. A bay horse was jumping, while a man on a black waited to jump next and then it was Jinny.

'Cheers,' the man said, smiling at Jinny. 'Not often we see an Arab. She's a beauty.'

The man's unexpected friendliness took Jinny by surprise. She bit hard into her bottom lip but couldn't stop it shaking. She wanted to tell him that Shantih was her horse but in a few hours time Mrs Raynor was coming to take her away, but when she tried to speak she had no words, only a dry, hard creaking.

The bay rode out of the ring with eight faults. The man rode in, his horse refused three times at the first jump and the man rode out.

Jinny's number was called. She closed her legs against Shantih's sides and rode into the brightness, knowing suddenly that she couldn't let Shantih down. She had to do her best. Gathering her horse together she cantered a circle and felt Shantih respond to her aids. Not fighting but paying attention and Jinny realised that there was not going to be a repeat performance of Gavinton. All the time she had spent schooling had not been wasted.

'You can jump them, jump them easily,' she whispered to Shantih, her being filled with the total confidence she usually knew when she was jumping Shantih.

A bell went and Jinny cantered through the start. Instantly a spread of poles loomed in front of her. Shantih cantered at it, taking off at exactly the right moment, so that Jinny was with her over the jump – soaring, landing as if she grew out of Shantih, was truly part of her horse.

All Jinny's fears had vanished. She was alive and real again and, as Shantih cleared the next upright, Jinny laughed aloud for delight. Crossed poles over a brush were cleared and left behind.

The tan muffling her hoofbeats, Shantih circled the ring. Tail lifted; her mane tongues of chestnut flame about her gleaming neck: her great eyes held the whole of the arena reflected in their liquid depths.

'A double,' thought Jinny, steadying Shantih before she pushed her on to rise, take six strides, and rise again, clearing the double with a sure rythmn that made it feel like one flowing jump. Ecstatically Jinny rode her at a post and rails. She felt Shantih gather herself for the leap and clear it. Somewhere a bell rang. Jinny hardly heard it as she raced to the brick wall. Insistent, the whistle was blown again and again, as a steward came running across the ring to Jinny.

'Wrong course,' he yelled. 'Disqualified. Sorry lass. Out.'

His words brought Jinny back to herself and as she swung Shantih round in front of the wall, not jumping it.

'What?' she demanded.

'Wrong course. You took the wrong course.' An elegant girl on a Roman-nosed cob came in to the ring.

Shantih shook her head, half rearing, refusing to leave

the ring, wanting to go on with this bright excitement of speed and flying.

'You would!' cried Nick as Jinny rode out. 'She was brilliant, splendiferous, and *you* mucked it all up. You stupid clot, you.' Nick's enraged face blazed up at Jinny. 'You saw the plan! You walked round the course. What on earth made you jump the post and rails? It wasn't even in a straight line from the double?'

Jinny slipped down from the saddle, made much of Shantih, then hid herself under the saddle flap, loosening Shantih's girths. She was totally disgusted with herself but brimming over with delight at Shantih's performance.

'You could have *WON*,' cried Nick. 'Nothing would have beaten her the way she was jumping in there. Nothing! And you had to go and muck it all up.'

'There's this afternoon,' Jinny said as they walked Shantih round to cool her off.

'Topscore! Huh! You've as much chance of winning that as you have of going to the moon. I only entered you for that because I thought you could jump the low score, easy jumps. Only for a practice. You haven't a chance in Topscore. Honestly you don't deserve a horse like Shantih!'

'Deserve her or not,' Jinny thought. 'She won't be mine much longer.'

Only a few grains of sand remained to trickle through the hourglass that timed her meeting with Mrs Raynor.

'At least,' thought Jinny. 'I'll have today,' for although she understood Nick's fury, knew she had been an idiot to have taken the wrong course, what mattered were the moments when time and space had been somewhere else; when there had only been Shantih and herself – soaring, flying – at one in the brightness of the arena.

'Let's watch for a bit,' said Nick when they had cooled Shantih off and settled her back into her box.

'Oke,' said Jinny, and they made their way to the arena to watch the jumping.

In the collecting ring, Mr Young was standing beside Liam mounted on Brandon.

'And I don't give a damn what you think,' Liam was shouting. 'You want me to win and this is the way I do it. So leave me alone.'

Liam's hard hat was pushed back on his head. He held Brandon in with a strangling rein and sat looking arrogantly down on the older man.

As Liam rode on Mr Young shook his head and, turning, recognised Nick.

'In two months,' he said ruefully, 'he has turned your little horse into a nervous wreck. I spend my money buying him horses to please his mother and this is what he does to them. Listen to advice? Never! He thinks of me as a senile geriatric, while he goes on ruining my horses.'

As Nick and Jinny sat down close to the entrance, Liam and Brandon were called into the ring.

'If I'd planned it I couldn't have timed it better,' said Nick bitterly, as Liam burst into the ring. Brandon's shoulders were already white with sweat and his mouth foamed.

Liam held him in as they galloped at the first jump, then released him to surge over it while he sat solid, hardly moving, ready to pull him back in again the second they landed and drive him on to the next fence.

Nick watched, never taking the knuckles of her clenched fist out of her mouth.

Twice Brandon's front legs sent poles crashing to the ground. Liam's heavy brows drew down and his mouth set in a clenched line as he galloped Brandon on at the wall. But Brandon came at it wrong. He would have stopped but Liam forced him to jump; sent him on, half leaping, half crashing, through the falling bricks. Brandon's nose brushed the ground. He struggled to keep his feet but Liam's unbalanced weight was too much for him and he slammed into the tan, throwing Liam over his head.

In seconds Brandon had splattered to his feet and stood staring about him until a steward caught his reins. But Liam didn't move. Two stewards dashed to him, Liam lifted his head, pointing to his leg, and when the stewards tried to help him to his feet his scream rang through the stadium. A stretcher was brought and Liam carried out as the next rider came in.

The steward led Brandon out of the ring and Nick ran forward.

'I know him,' she said. 'I'll take him.'

She took Brandon and led him outside. Whispering, talking gently to him she searched his legs for any injuries and, watching her, Jinny knew that her cynicism had all been a mask. In her own way Nick cared for Brandon every bit as much as Jinny did for Shantih. Only Nick was so much better at keeping her mask close to her skin.

'Good, good,' said Mr Young, hurrying across with his short-strided, groom's run. 'You've got him. I'll need to go with the boy. Broken his leg. Need to get him to hospital.'

'Serve him right if he'd broken his neck. You shouldn't let him ride when he treats horses like that.' All Nick's suffering and hurt were in her voice.

'He's my only grandchild,' said Mr Young, his voice agreeing with Nick. 'You're right. You're right. Does well enough on the carthorses he usually rides. Your nag's too good for him. Still, still, got to get him X-rayed. Box 43. Will you see to Brandon?'

'Course,' said Nick, and Mr Young hurried away.

'You'd better let Aunt Ag know what's happened,' suggested Nick wanting to be by herself with Brandon.

Before Jinny went back she studied the Plan of the Course for the Topscore competition. The jumps were numbered from 10, the lowest score and easiest fence, to 120 points for the highest fence. The points for each fence jumped clear were added together to give each competitor's score. An upright fence known as the Joker was valued at 200 points but Jinny knew from reading Nick's rule book, that if the Joker was knocked down, 200 points were subtracted from the competitor's score.

'Thought we could jump the lowest!' scorned Jinny. The high of her morning's jumping was glowing in her mind. She would jump the highest jumps. Make her course over the highest jumps including the Joker. She studied the plan with total concentration.

To take in the highest numbers Shantih would need to turn and twist, sure as a minnow. But Jinny knew she could do it. Having watched the jumping at Gavinton and at Ardair that morning, she knew how much more nimble Shantih was than the other horses. Shantih could turn in her own length, spin round on a halfpence. All the galloping and leaping on the Finmory moors which was second nature to Shantih had increased her Arab sureness until she could turn and twist with faultless certainty.

The turn between the parallel poles, rated at 120, and the Joker for 200 was so tight that Jinny was certain that other horses wouldn't risk it: but Shantih could.

Pinned beside the Course Plan was the results of the draw for placings in Topscore. Jinny was second last to jump, which meant she would know the score she had to beat.

The Topscore competition was at half-past two. By the time Jinny started to get Shantih ready Nick had still not returned, but Steph had been second in her class and folded in her jacket pocket was a blue rosette to prove it.

Richard helped Jinny to tack up and mount.

'Thanks very much,' she said, glad to have his reassuring presence.

'If Nick hasn't surfaced I'll hold her for you while you walk the course,' he promised. 'And this time make sure you know where you're going.'

'I am sure,' said Jinny, and as she walked and trotted Shantih in the exercising area she went over and over the fences she was going to jump. There would be no mistakes this time.

It was afternoon now. Every stranger Jinny saw might be Mrs Raynor. If she was not here already she would be on her way, drawing closer with every minute.

'But you have been mine,' Jinny told Shantih. 'She will come and claim you and take you away. You will be Wildfire of Talisker again. But you have truly been Shantih. Have been truly mine.'

There was still no sign of Nick when Richard came to hold Shantih while Jinny walked the course.

'She must have settled in with Brandon,' Richard said, taking Shantih's reins.

'Shouldn't be surprised if she's horsenapped him, after seeing Liam riding him like that,' Jinny said as she went into the arena.

This time she paid no attention to the other riders. She marked out the course she was going to ride. What the others did was up to themselves. Jinny knew the fences that she and Shantih were going to jump.

Walking the Pathfinders course, the jumps had seemed enormous. The highest-scoring jumps in the Topscore competition were far higher than any in the Pathfinders, yet Jinny was only concerned with the distances between them and the tightness of the turns. Landing from the spread that was worth 120 points, Shantih would need to be at an angle, stop dead, spin on her hocks and after one stride take off to clear the upright gate that was the Joker.

'Only an Arab could do it,' thought Jinny, and as she stared at the gate there was not the slightest doubt in her mind. Shantih would clear the Joker.

Richard waited in the collecting ring with Jinny, telling her the scores the other riders had made. When her number was called to go into the waiting area, the lowest score was 500 and the highest 980. The woman in front of Jinny rode her grey into the ring and Jinny was next.

'We'll do it,' Jinny whispered to Shantih. 'Be ready. Be listening to me.'

Shantih flicked one ear backwards to the sound of Jinny's voice.

'Fast as the wind,' said Jinny. 'It's the last time. Make it the best.' And the course they would jump was electrified for their coming.

Jinny glanced across at the spectator's entrance, wondering what had happened to Nick, and there, coming into the stadium, was Miss Trevor, still wearing her green County uniform.

A strange woman walked at her side, broad shouldered as she was tall. Her hair must once have been as red as Jinny's own but now it was streaked with savage slashes of white. Her face was drawn into wrinkles like cooling skin on boiled milk. Under bushy eyebrows, huge amber eyes stared about her. She was wearing a loose coat of moss green tweed and a wool dress to match; her knee high boots were made of fine black leather.

The woman saw Shantih. Her whole face lit up, her great eyes shone and she started forward towards Jinny.

'Wildfire!' she cried and the bell went to call Jinny into the ring.

Jinny eased her fingers on the reins, sat forward and felt Shantih's pent-up energy burst forward into speed. Jinny's mind was one-pointed, with a single aim – to jump the course she had marked out for herself.

Through the start she went and Shantih was storming, was fire. A smallish spread jump that Jinny had not counted on appeared in front of them and was left behind under Shantih's flying hooves and they rode straight at 80 – a brush fence. In mid-air Jinny touched her right rein and Shantih landed to cross to the right and soar over poles for 90.

The crossed poles for 100 had to be taken at an angle. Shantih leapt, stretched diagonally across the jump and landed close, too close, to parallel poles worth 60 points. Jinny had not intended to jump it but she had no choice, their speed carried her on and over. The top pole clattered to the ground but Jinny was hardly aware of it for in two strides Shantih was at the take-off for 120 – a spread that seemed to reach out over half the arena, seemed to rise like the flow of a fountain as Jinny put Shantih at it. She was held in an intensity of effort, a total concentration that shut everything else out except the ecstatic daring of her horse, the challenge of the jumps and her own will.

After the spread for 120 Shantih must stop dead, spin round and after only one stride clear the white-gate Joker.

'Now, Shantih. Now!' Jinny cried, checking her. From her galloping stride Shantih stopped dead, swung round and the Joker was ahead.

Jinny felt Shantih gather herself for the all but impossible leap; felt her sink on her quarters, spring vertically upwards from her hocks and reach for the top of the gate. She screwed over it with Jinny sitting tight as a limpet. There was the sound of hooves against wood but almost unconsciously Jinny knew from the crowds exhalation that the gate – the Joker – had not fallen.

'Go on, go on,' praised Jinny as she swung Shantih round and for a second time rode her at the brush fence for 80.

There was no resistance in Shantih, only delight that she should go on soaring and leaping. The brush, the upright poles, the crossed poles were behind them for a second round and time hot breathing at their heels. The Joker waited, mocking, could not be jumped twice by this mad Arab and her demented rider.

They rolled over the spread for a second 120, as if a wave carried them. As she arched downwards Jinny felt Shantih alert to spin round and rise over the Joker. So swift was her halt, so sudden her turn that without any encouragement from Jinny, she lifted over it – pricked ears, urgent eyes. Her forefeet touched down and the bell went. They had cleared the Joker twice. A thunder of applause roared around them as they galloped through the finish and out of the ring.

'We did it!' Jinny cried. 'Oh Shantih, Shantih! Oh Horse!'

Jinny flung herself to the ground and threw her arms round Shantih's neck, breathing in the strong, sweet stench of sweating chestnut horse. This last ride had been the best. The one ride against which all future achievements would be measured and found wanting.

Jinny loosened Shantih's girths, and taking her reins over her head began to walk her round the exercise area.

'One thousand, two hundred and forty!!! Can she jump!' shouted Richard. 'Never have I seen anything like that in my life before.'

'It was only for once,' said Jinny. 'Once only because it was our last time together.' And she turned to face Miss Trevor and Mrs Raynor.

'Congratulations, my dear,' said Mrs Raynor and her voice was gravel. She held out a hand mis-shapen with arthritis. 'You jumped brilliantly. And Wildfire! I coud hardly believe my eyes. She flew for you.'

Miss Trevor twitched her nose and introduced Mrs Raynor.

The huge amber eyes looked straight at Jinny.

'She is my Wildfire. So like her mother.' Mrs Raynor's twisted hands caressed Shantih's face and neck. 'It's so wonderful to see her again. I never thought it possible. We had nearly given up hope, you know, but that you should never do.'

After the glory of Shantih's jumping Jinny was lost in a sudden desolation. There was only Shantih, herself and Mrs Raynor left in the whole world. Nothing else mattered, and she must give Shantih back to Mrs Raynor; for Jinny knew that Mrs Raynor loved Shantih as much as she did. All the time Shantih had been at Finmory Mrs Raynor had been grieving for her.

Jinny held out Shantih's reins to her. She wanted to say, 'I'm glad you've found her,' but couldn't.

Mrs Raynor looked down at Jinny's outstretched hand.

'You've won,' Richard roared, dashing across to them. 'You beat them all. Up you get. Ride her in for your winnings.' He bustled Jinny back into the saddle.

Dazed. Jinny stood at the head of a line of six horses, all ridden by adults, whose expressions varied from smiling amazement to open hostility.

A group of officials came towards them, a lady pinned the red rosette to Shantih's bridle, praised Jinny's riding and Shantih's jumping. Jinny wanted to tell her that it had been for the one time only. Could never have happened before; could never happen again. It had been a celebration of her love for Shantih.

'Give them a gallop round,' the man who had been second said, laughing down at Jinny from the height of his seventeen hand bay, and Jinny realised that they were waiting for her to lead the way.

As Jinny touched Shantih into a gallop the applause rose about them. The hooves of the six other horses thundered behind them and Shantih flew faster than the whirlwind; was light and fire compared to the dull beasts that pounded behind her.

And in their circling there came to Jinny an acceptance of what had to be, the inevitable, for Mrs Raynor had bred Shantih, had reared her and loved her long before Jinny had known her.

They galloped round the ring twice. Then a steward shouted, 'Take the Arab round again,' and Shantih danced her way round a third time.

'Now,' thought Jinny. 'Now. The applause, the red rosette, the spotlights, the crowd, they are all mine; and for a last time, Shantih is mine.'

When she rode out into the open air she was half blinded by the light. She slid down from Shantih and walked, blinking against the sun, to where she could just make out Mrs Raynor and Miss Trevor.

'She's yours,' said Jinny, looking up at the blazing

saffron eyes and the streaked hair of Mrs Raynor. 'I'm glad you found her.' And again Jinny held out Shantih's reins to her.

'I told you, she's been eating her heart out ever since she got your letter.' It was Petra's voice.

Jinny looked round in astonishment. All her family were there.

'What . . .' began Jinny, suddenly remembering that her mother had said they would be there.

'We had to come,' said her father. We couldn't leave you to deal with this by yourself. Then we had a puncture. Only got here a few minutes ago. Didn't see you jumping but we've met Mrs Raynor.'

'It's all right,' said her mother, smiling at Jinny.

Mrs Raynor laid both her hands on Jinny's, pressing Jinny's hand tightly on to Shantih's rein.

'What else could I have done?' she demanded. 'Without seeing you? Without seeing Wildfire? I couldn't have written to say she was yours until I'd met you, but of course she's yours. The Wildfire that was stolen from my stud hadn't even been broken in. You have made Shantih what she is today. She is your horse.'

Jinny's heart somersaulted into her throat. For seconds she could not believe her ears. 'She is your horse,' rang her like a bell.

Mrs Raynor lifted her hands from Jinny's and Jinny flung herself into her arms, hands round her neck, and Mrs Raynor held her tightly.

'So thoughtless of me,' she said. 'I should have come up to see her when I got your letter. Forgive me.'

Suddenly everyone was talking at once, praising Shantih and questioning Mrs Raynor.

'Saw you jump. Out of this world!' Nick was back with them.

'It was for once only,' said Jinny. 'We could never do it again,' and she was stricken to think of her own joy, when Brandon had been taken away from Nick.

'I've to keep Shantih! Mrs Raynor has given her to me! And you can ride her whenever you like.'

'You won't mean that tomorrow,' mocked Nick, laughing at Jinny. 'Anyway it's O.K. I've got a better horse to ride. It's all fixed. Mr Young is back from the hospital. Liam's leg will be in plaster for two months, so I've to ride Brandon, jump him at all the shows. Not just while Liam is plastered but for good. He's never going to let Liam ride him again. And I've to work for Mr Young – weekends, holidays, the lot.' Nick's ear to ear grin matched Jinny's own.

When they had watched Richard jump to fourth place in his class they all went back to Finmory where Jinny told Mrs Raynor some of the things that had happened to Shantih since she had found her, and Mrs Raynor talked about her stud and passed round photographs of Shantih, calling her Wildfire, but it didn't matter now.

'Don't believe it,' thought Jinny, gazing round the room. 'Can't believe it is all over.' She pinched herself hard but nothing changed. The nightmare of losing Shantih was over.

It was well after midnight before the Websters, Nick, Miss Trevor and Mrs Raynor went away. Leaving her family sitting round the table over a last cup of coffee, Jinny walked down through the silent night to the stables. In the beam of Jinny's torch Shantih lay fast asleep. At Jinny's approach she lifted her head, whickered a welcome and got to her feet.

'Most dear horse,' said Jinny. 'My most dear Shantih.' And Shantih walked across the box, stretched out her sleek neck and clipped face to breathe over Jinny.

'Not even the ringmaster can take you away from me now,' Jinny said. 'You are mine forever.'